BATMAN

THE BRAVE AND THE BOLD®

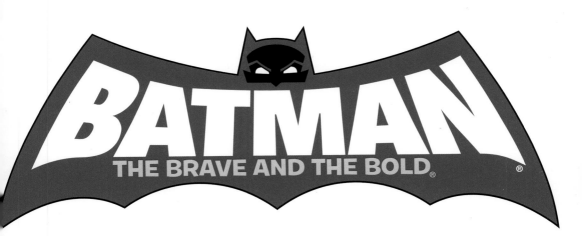

STONE ARCH BOOKS
a capstone imprint

STONE ARCH BOOKS™
Published in 2012
A Capstone Imprint
1710 Roe Crest Drive
North Mankato, MN 56003
www.capstonepub.com

DC Comics
1700 Broadway, New York, NY 10019
A Warner Bros. Entertainment Company

Originally published by DC Comics in the U.S. in single magazine form as Batman: The Brave and the Bold #2.

Cataloging-in-Publication Data is available at the Library of Congress website:
ISBN: 978-1-4342-4546-5 (library binding)

Summary: Why are trolls and ogres from a video game raiding the real world? It's up to Batman and Blue Beetle to find out - and they discover that someone's not just playing around!

STONE ARCH BOOKS
Ashley C. Andersen Zantop *Publisher*
Michael Dahl *Editorial Director*
Donald Lemke & Christianne Jones *Editors*
Heather Kindseth *Creative Director*
Hilary Wacholz *Designer*
Kathy McColley *Production Specialist*

DC COMICS
Rachel Gluckstern & Michael Siglain *Original U.S. Editors*
Harvey Richards *U.S. Assistant Editor*
James Tucker *Cover Artist*

Printed in the United States of America in Brainerd, Minnesota.
122012 007078R

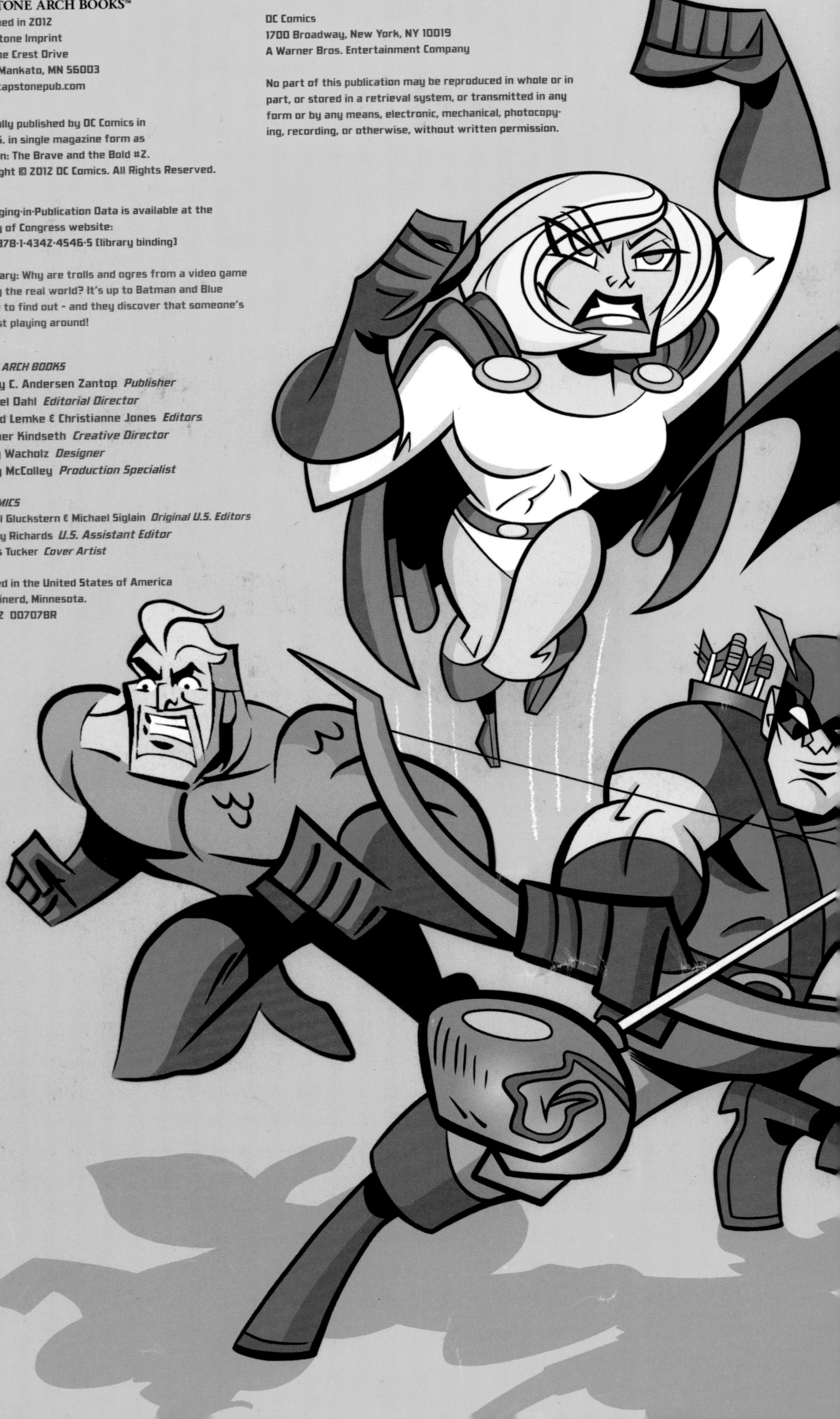

BATMAN
THE BRAVE AND THE BOLD®

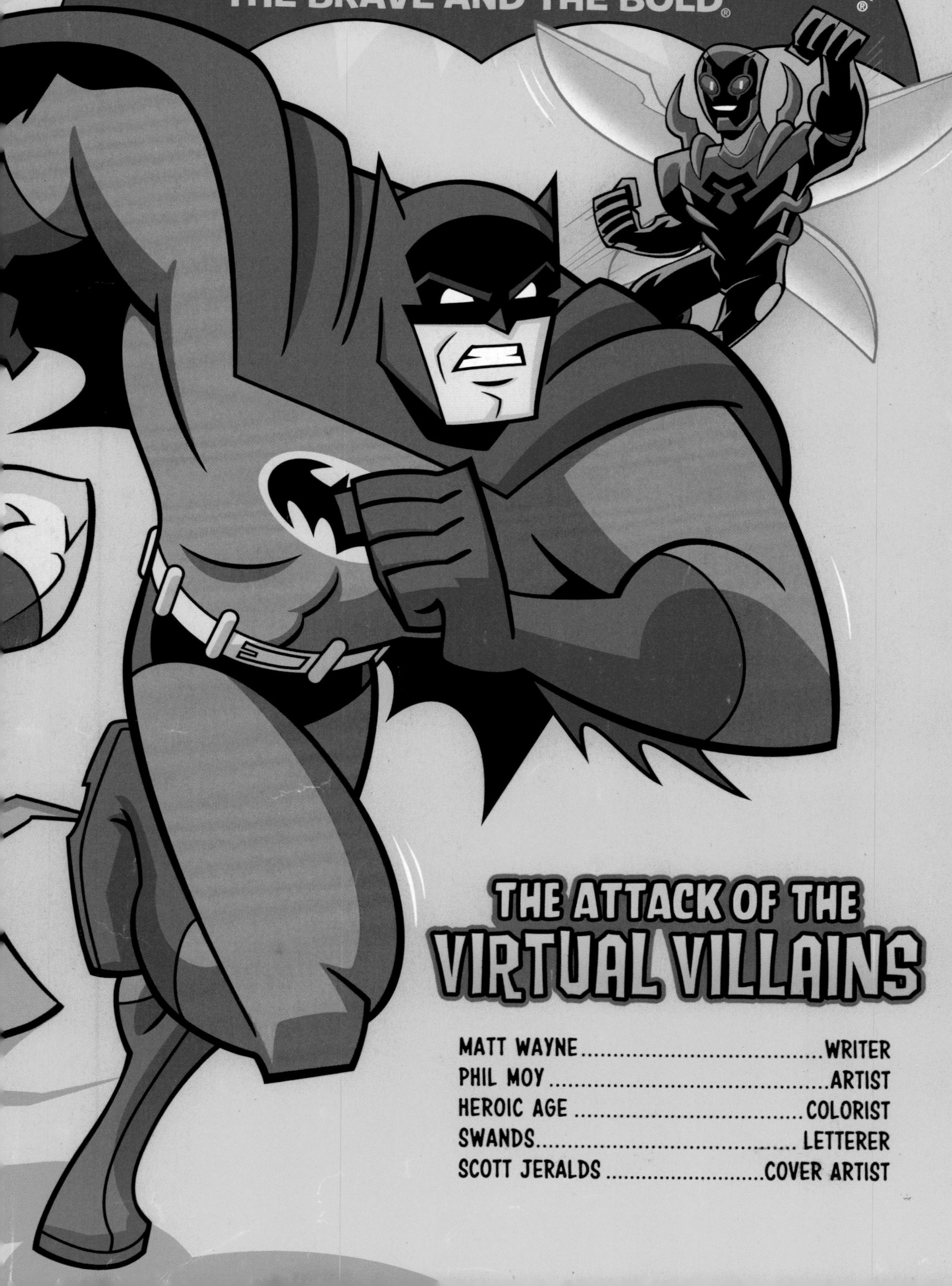

THE ATTACK OF THE VIRTUAL VILLAINS

MATT WAYNE .... WRITER
PHIL MOY .... ARTIST
HEROIC AGE .... COLORIST
SWANDS .... LETTERER
SCOTT JERALDS .... COVER ARTIST

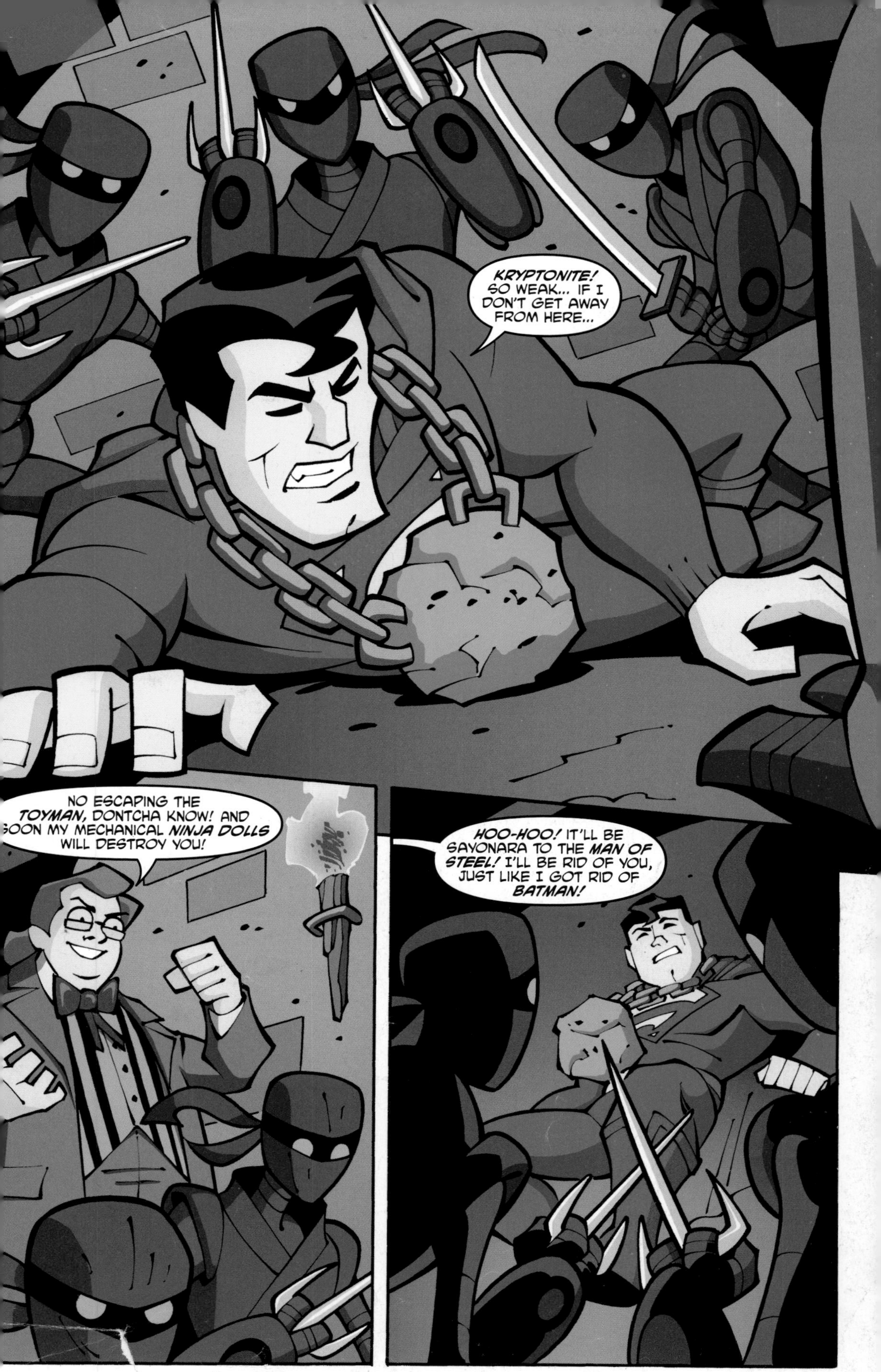
KRYPTONITE! SO WEAK... IF I DON'T GET AWAY FROM HERE...
NO ESCAPING THE TOYMAN, DONTCHA KNOW! AND SOON MY MECHANICAL NINJA DOLLS WILL DESTROY YOU!
HOO-HOO! IT'LL BE SAYONARA TO THE MAN OF STEEL! I'LL BE RID OF YOU, JUST LIKE I GOT RID OF BATMAN!

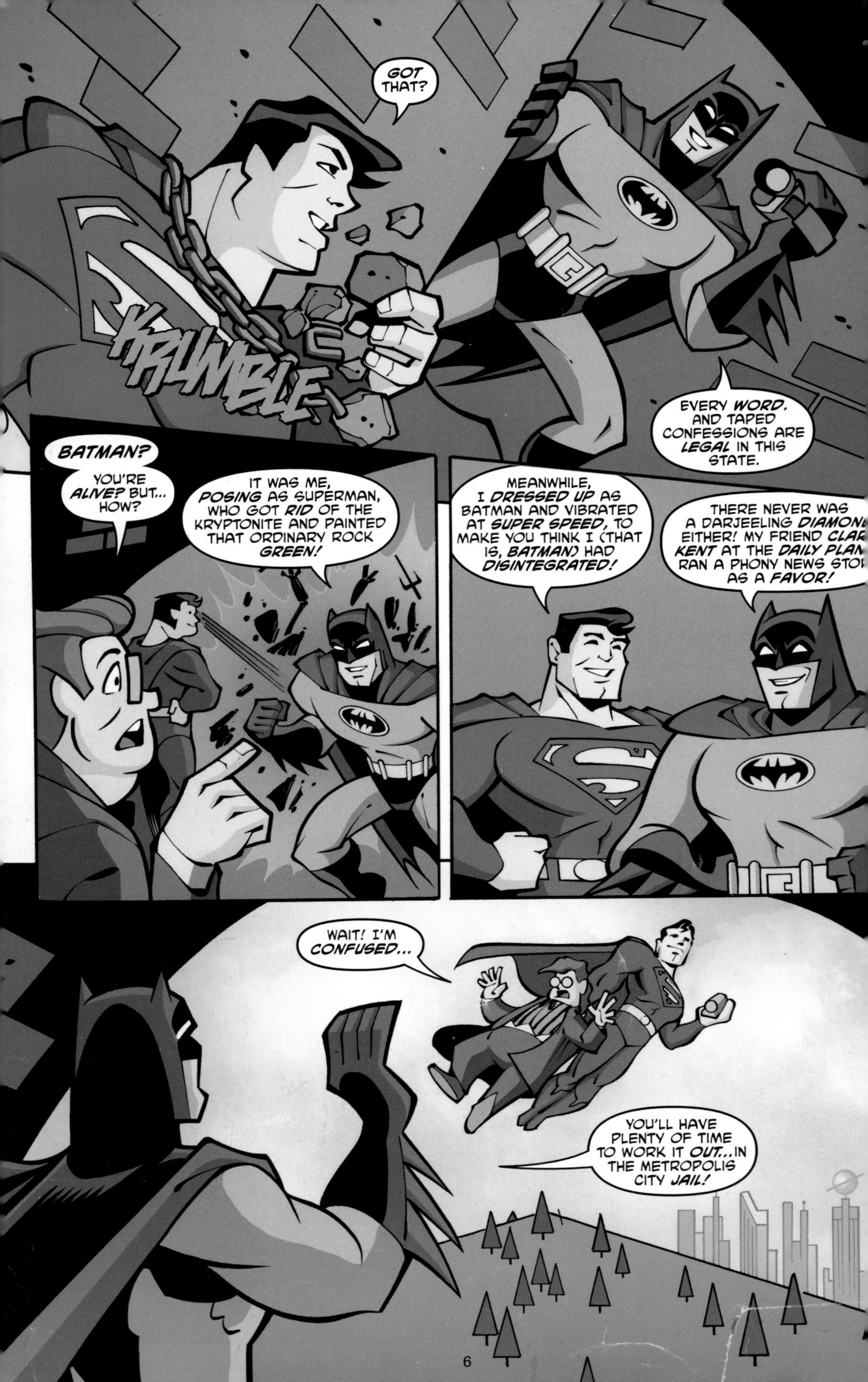
GOT THAT?
KRUMBLE
EVERY WORD. AND TAPED CONFESSIONS ARE LEGAL IN THIS STATE.
BATMAN?
YOU'RE ALIVE? BUT... HOW?
IT WAS ME, POSING AS SUPERMAN, WHO GOT RID OF THE KRYPTONITE AND PAINTED THAT ORDINARY ROCK GREEN!
MEANWHILE, I DRESSED UP AS BATMAN AND VIBRATED AT SUPER SPEED, TO MAKE YOU THINK I (THAT IS, BATMAN) HAD DISINTEGRATED!
THERE NEVER WAS A DARJEELING DIAMON EITHER! MY FRIEND CLAR KENT AT THE DAILY PLAN RAN A PHONY NEWS STOR AS A FAVOR!
WAIT! I'M CONFUSED...
YOU'LL HAVE PLENTY OF TIME TO WORK IT OUT...IN THE METROPOLIS CITY JAIL!

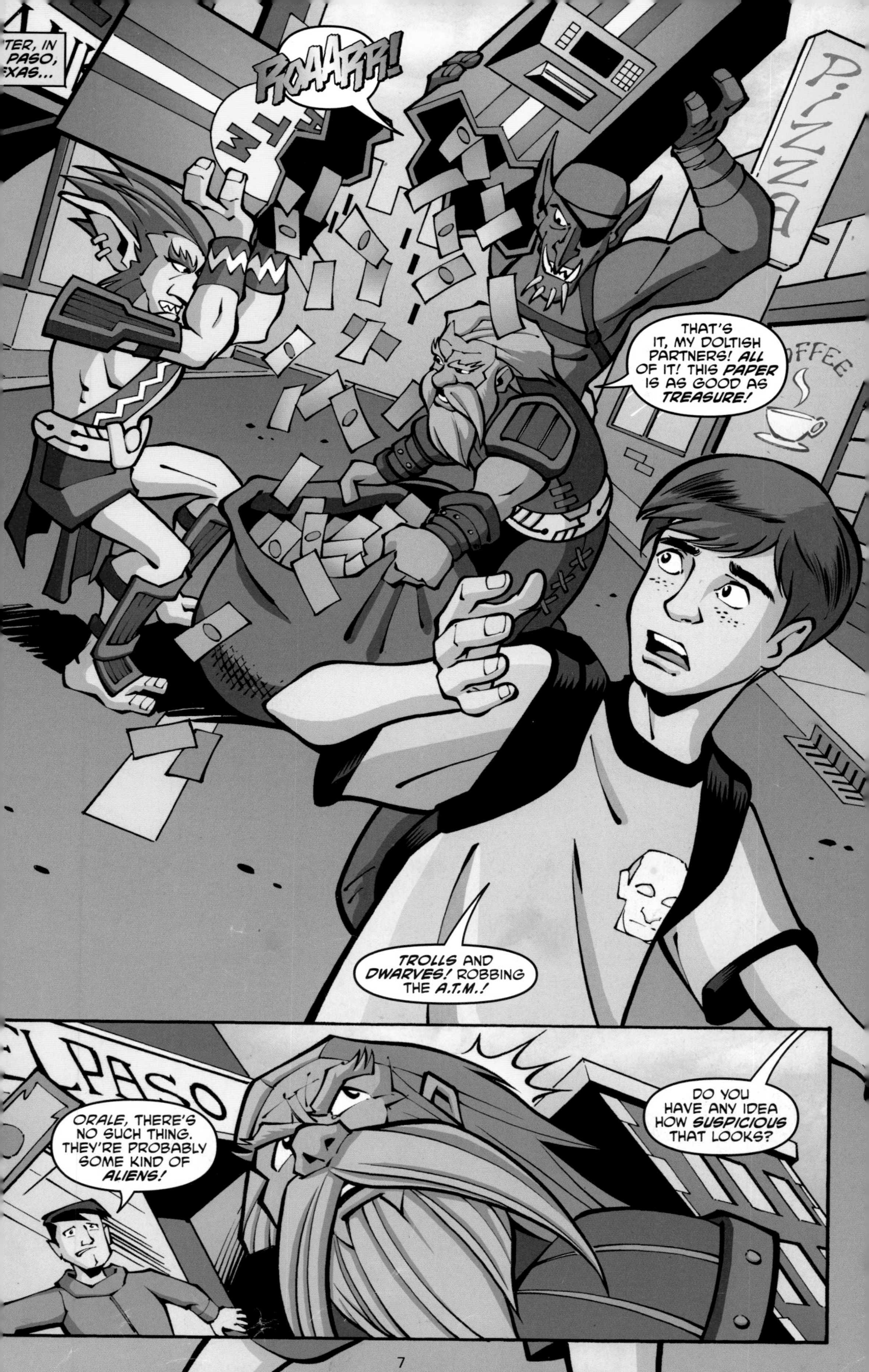
TER, IN
PASO,
EXAS...
ROAAARR!
ATM
THAT'S IT, MY DOLTISH PARTNERS! ALL OF IT! THIS PAPER IS AS GOOD AS TREASURE!
PIZZA
OFFEE
TROLLS AND DWARVES! ROBBING THE A.T.M.!
EL PASO
ORALE, THERE'S NO SUCH THING. THEY'RE PROBABLY SOME KIND OF ALIENS!
DO YOU HAVE ANY IDEA HOW SUSPICIOUS THAT LOOKS?

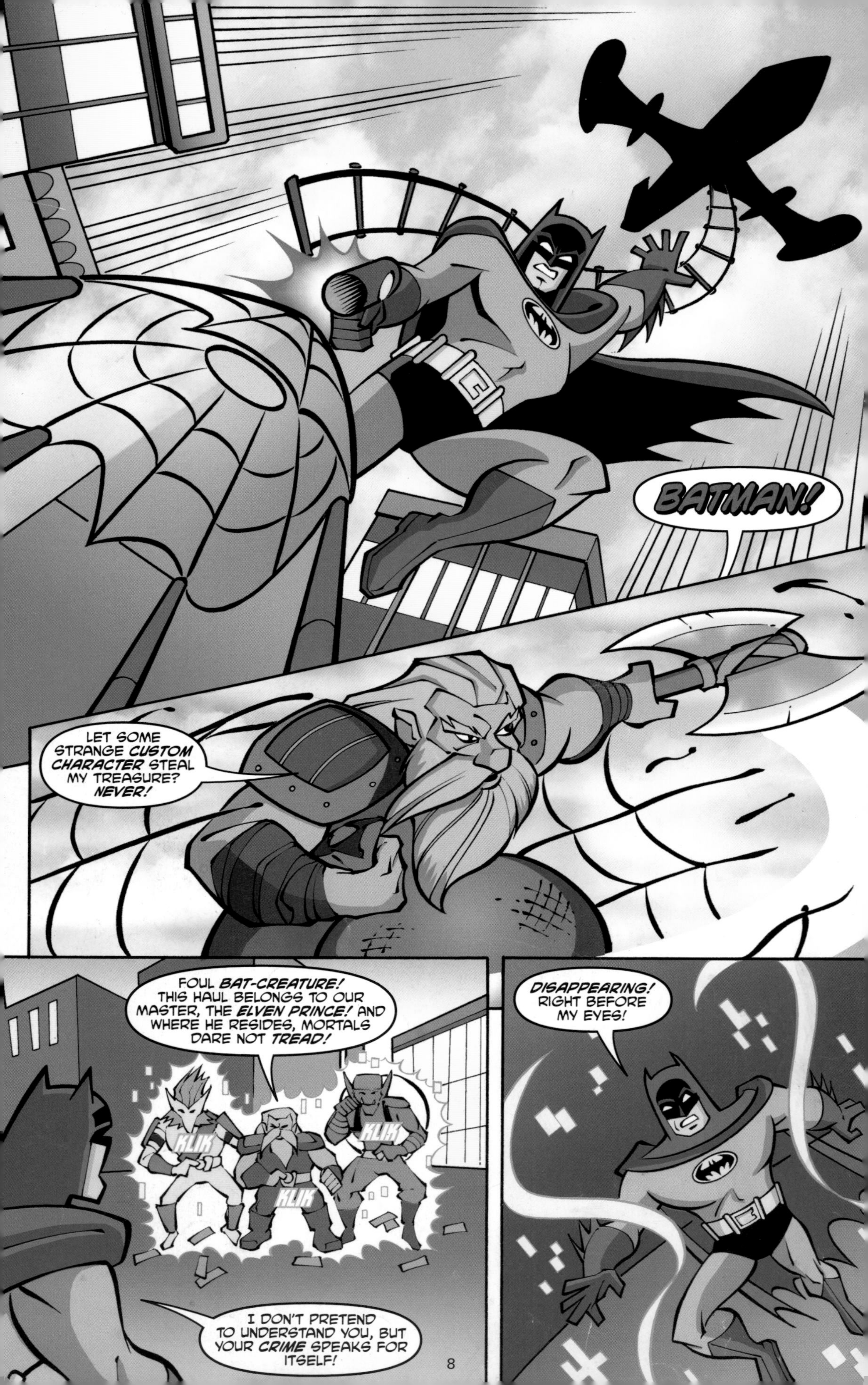
BATMAN!
LET SOME STRANGE CUSTOM CHARACTER STEAL MY TREASURE? NEVER!
FOUL BAT-CREATURE! THIS HAUL BELONGS TO OUR MASTER, THE ELVEN PRINCE! AND WHERE HE RESIDES, MORTALS DARE NOT TREAD!
KLIK
KLIK
KLIK
I DON'T PRETEND TO UNDERSTAND YOU, BUT YOUR CRIME SPEAKS FOR ITSELF!
DISAPPEARING! RIGHT BEFORE MY EYES!

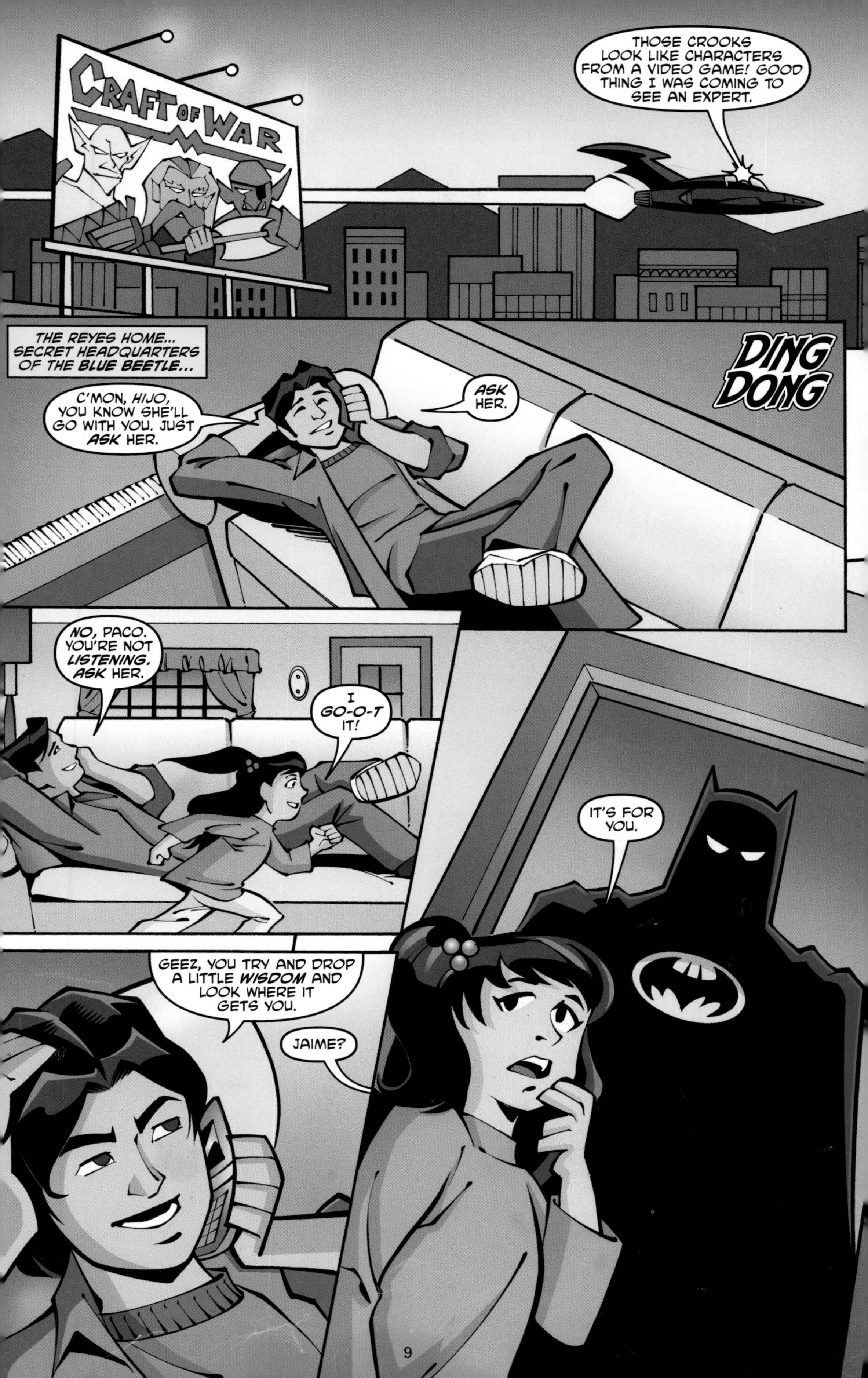

THOSE CROOKS LOOK LIKE CHARACTERS FROM A VIDEO GAME! GOOD THING I WAS COMING TO SEE AN EXPERT.
CRAFT OF WAR
THE REYES HOME... SECRET HEADQUARTERS OF THE BLUE BEETLE...
C'MON, HIJO, YOU KNOW SHE'LL GO WITH YOU. JUST ASK HER.
ASK HER.
DING DONG
NO, PACO. YOU'RE NOT LISTENING. ASK HER.
I GO-O-T IT!
IT'S FOR YOU.
GEEZ, YOU TRY AND DROP A LITTLE WISDOM AND LOOK WHERE IT GETS YOU.
JAIME?

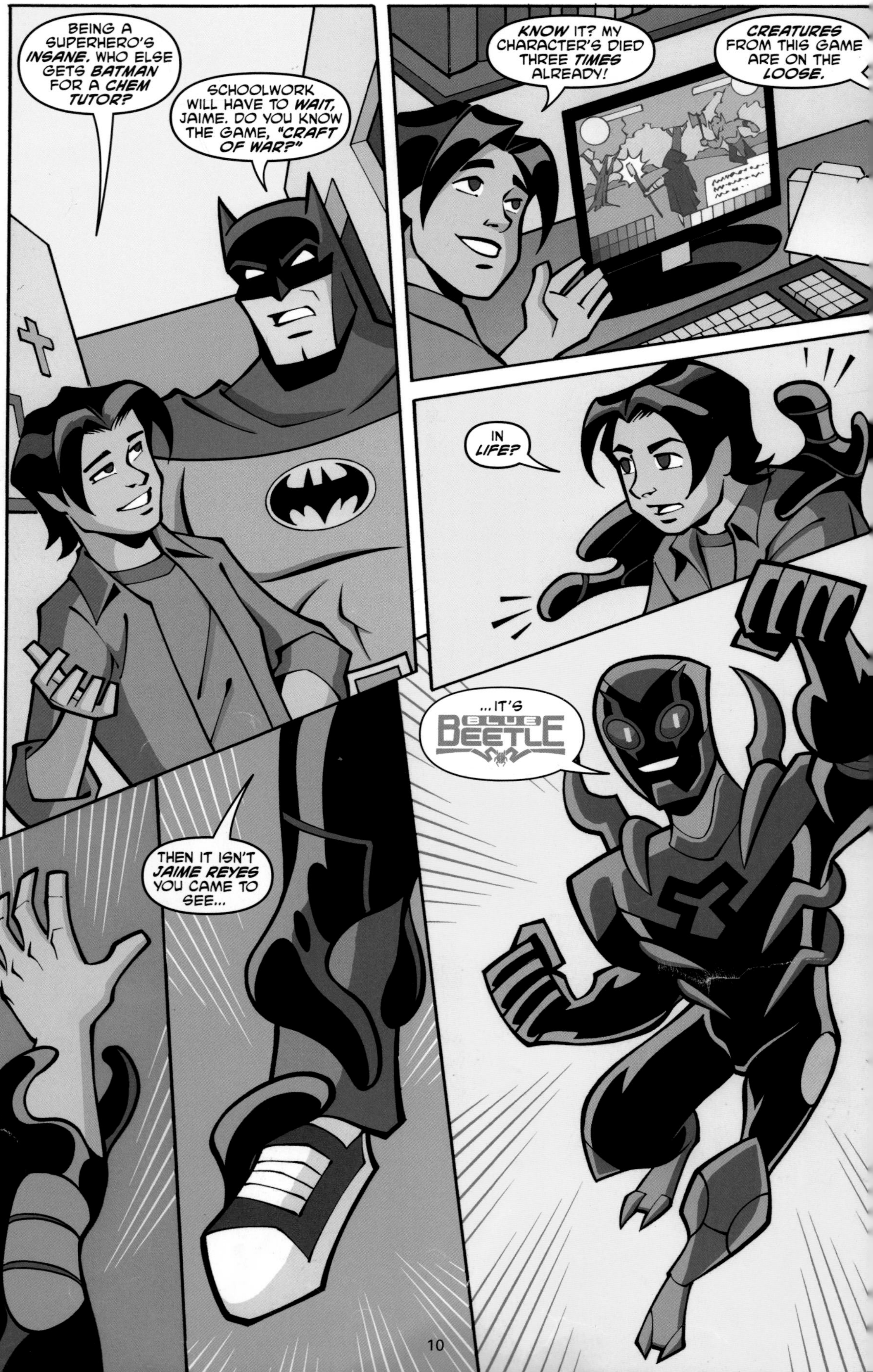
BEING A SUPERHERO'S INSANE. WHO ELSE GETS BATMAN FOR A CHEM TUTOR?
SCHOOLWORK WILL HAVE TO WAIT, JAIME. DO YOU KNOW THE GAME, "CRAFT OF WAR?"
KNOW IT? MY CHARACTER'S DIED THREE TIMES ALREADY!
CREATURES FROM THIS GAME ARE ON THE LOOSE.
IN LIFE?
THEN IT ISN'T JAIME REYES YOU CAME TO SEE...
...IT'S BLUE BEETLE

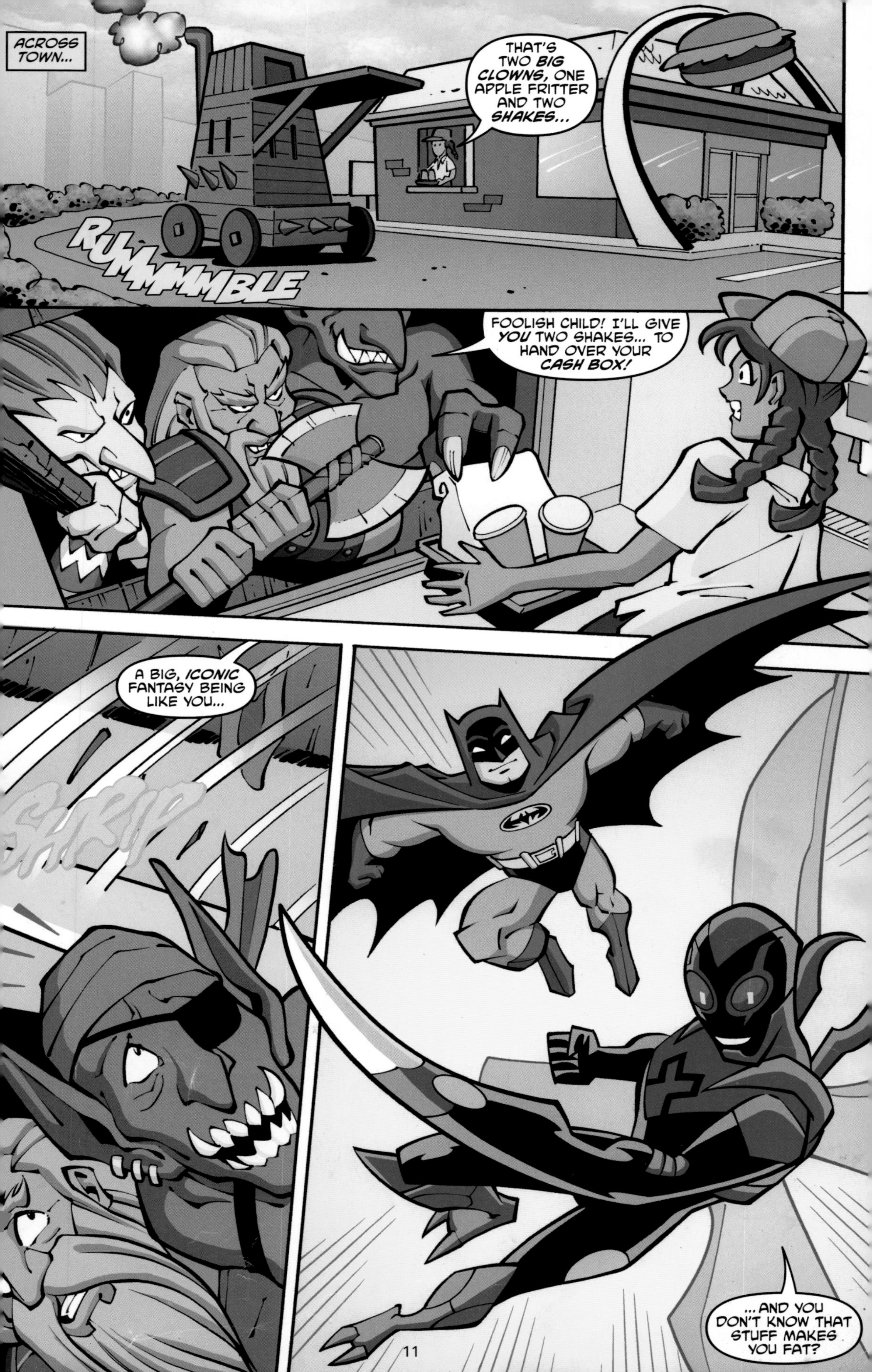
ACROSS TOWN...
THAT'S TWO BIG CLOWNS, ONE APPLE FRITTER AND TWO SHAKES...
RUMMMMMBLE
FOOLISH CHILD! I'LL GIVE YOU TWO SHAKES... TO HAND OVER YOUR CASH BOX!
A BIG, ICONIC FANTASY BEING LIKE YOU...
SHRIP
...AND YOU DON'T KNOW THAT STUFF MAKES YOU FAT?

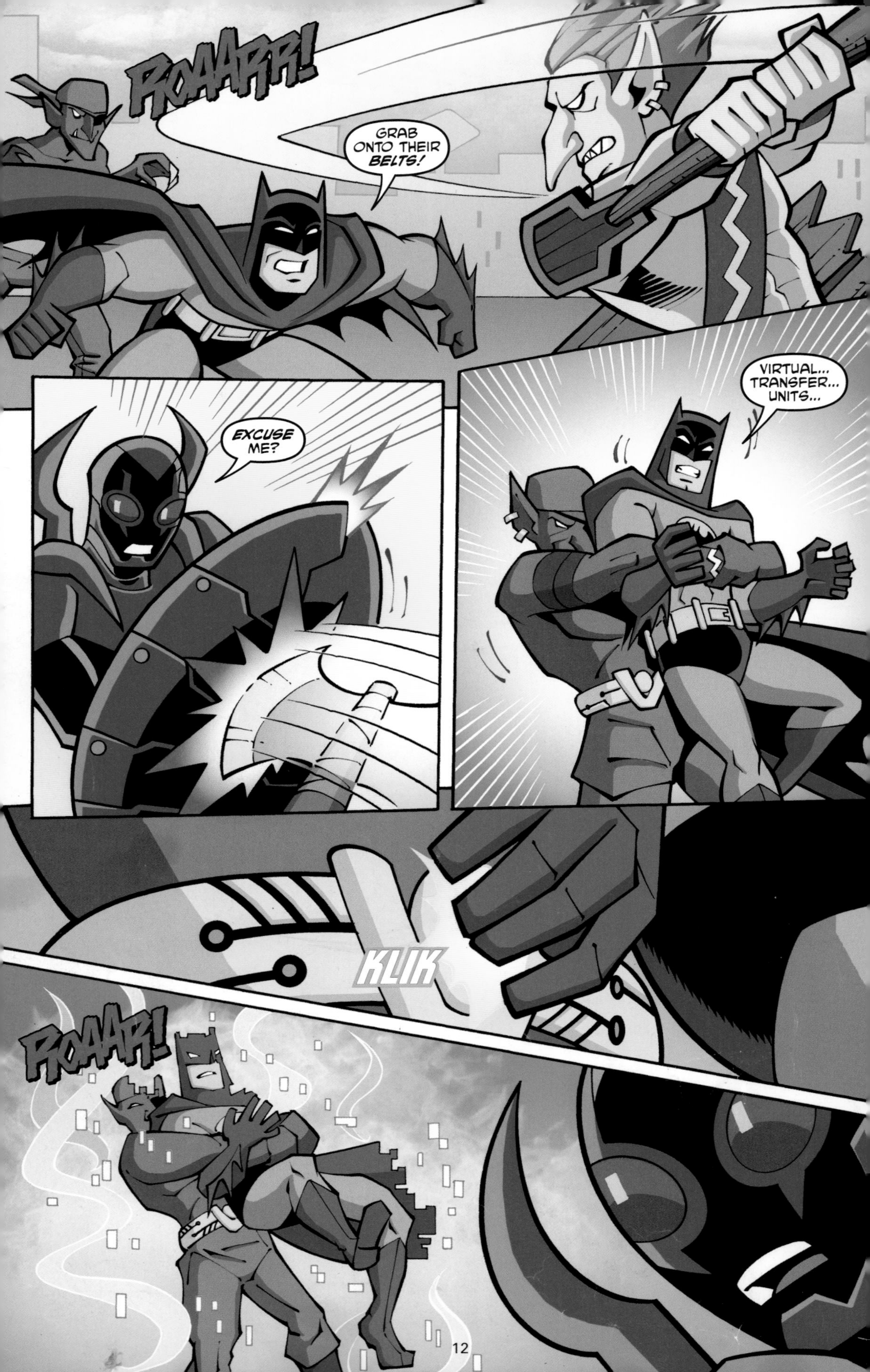

ROAARR!
GRAB ONTO THEIR BELTS!
EXCUSE ME?
VIRTUAL... TRANSFER... UNITS...
KLIK
ROAAR!

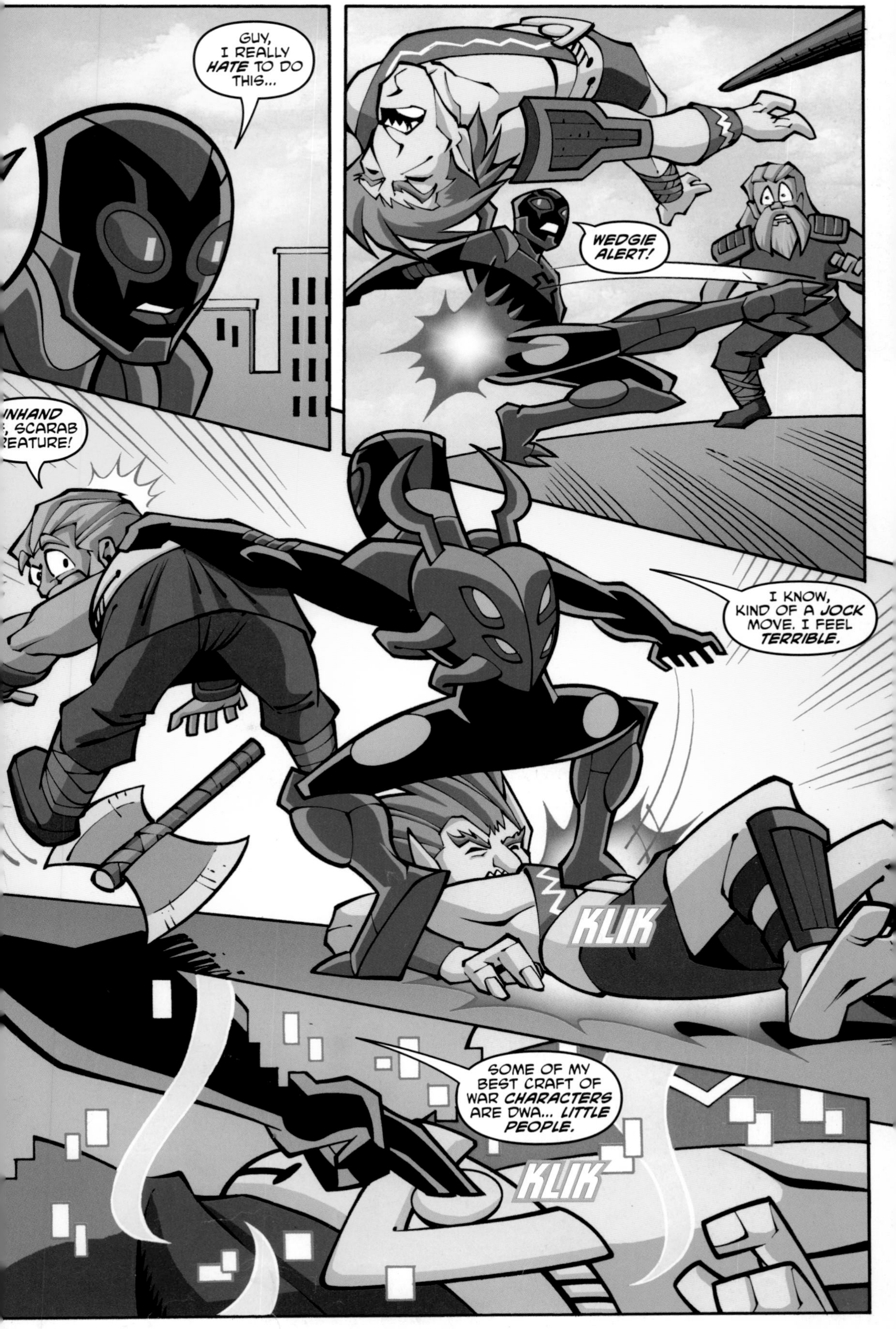
GUY, I REALLY HATE TO DO THIS...
WEDGIE ALERT!
UNHAND E, SCARAB REATURE!
I KNOW, KIND OF A JOCK MOVE. I FEEL TERRIBLE.
KLIK
SOME OF MY BEST CRAFT OF WAR CHARACTERS ARE DWA... LITTLE PEOPLE.
KLIK

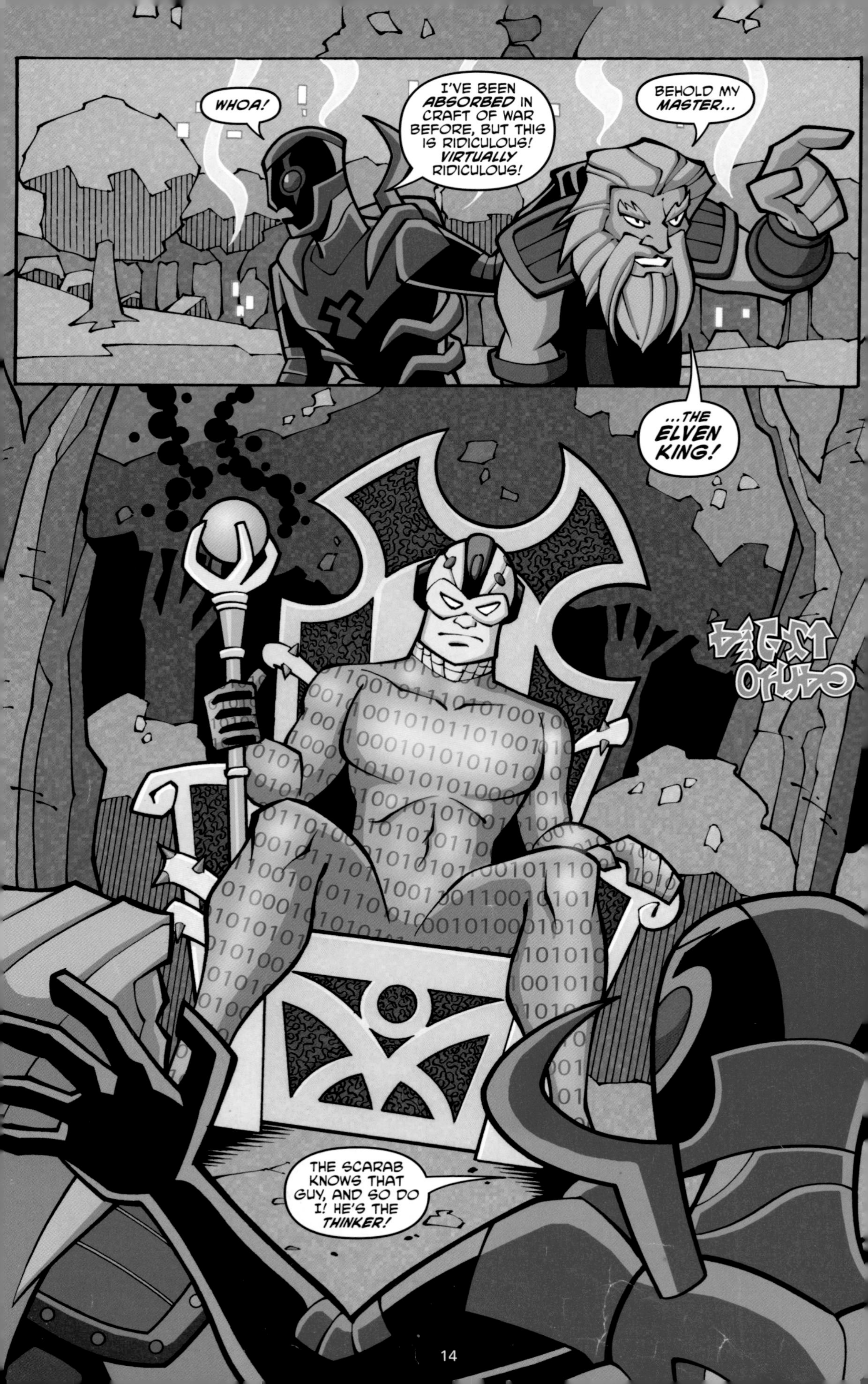
WHOA!
I'VE BEEN ABSORBED IN CRAFT OF WAR BEFORE, BUT THIS IS RIDICULOUS! VIRTUALLY RIDICULOUS!
BEHOLD MY MASTER...
...THE ELVEN KING!
THE SCARAB KNOWS THAT GUY, AND SO DO I! HE'S THE THINKER!

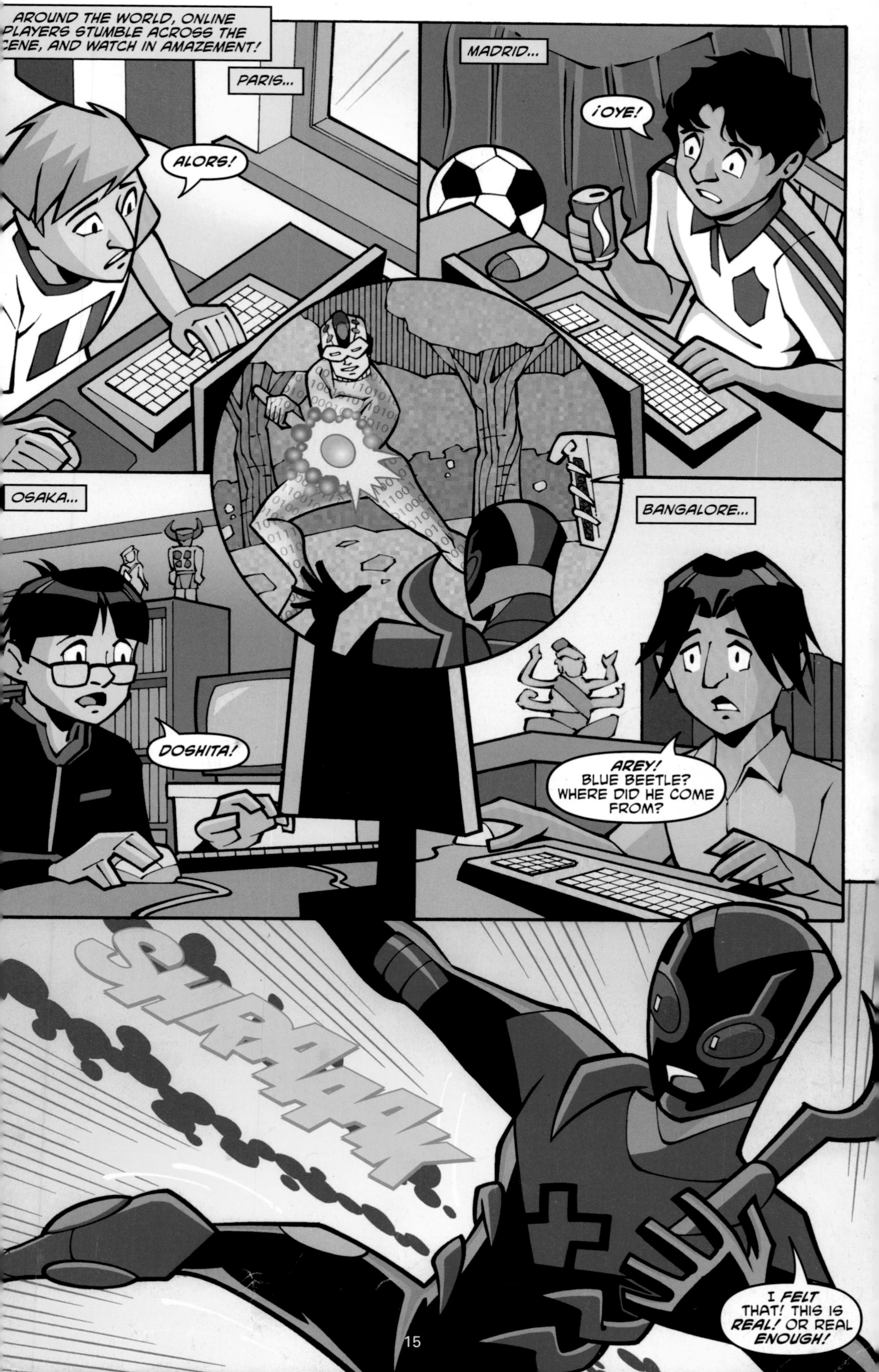

AROUND THE WORLD, ONLINE PLAYERS STUMBLE ACROSS THE SCENE, AND WATCH IN AMAZEMENT!
PARIS...
ALORS!
MADRID...
¡OYE!
OSAKA...
DOSHITA!
BANGALORE...
AREY! BLUE BEETLE? WHERE DID HE COME FROM?
SHRAAK
I FELT THAT! THIS IS REAL! OR REAL ENOUGH!

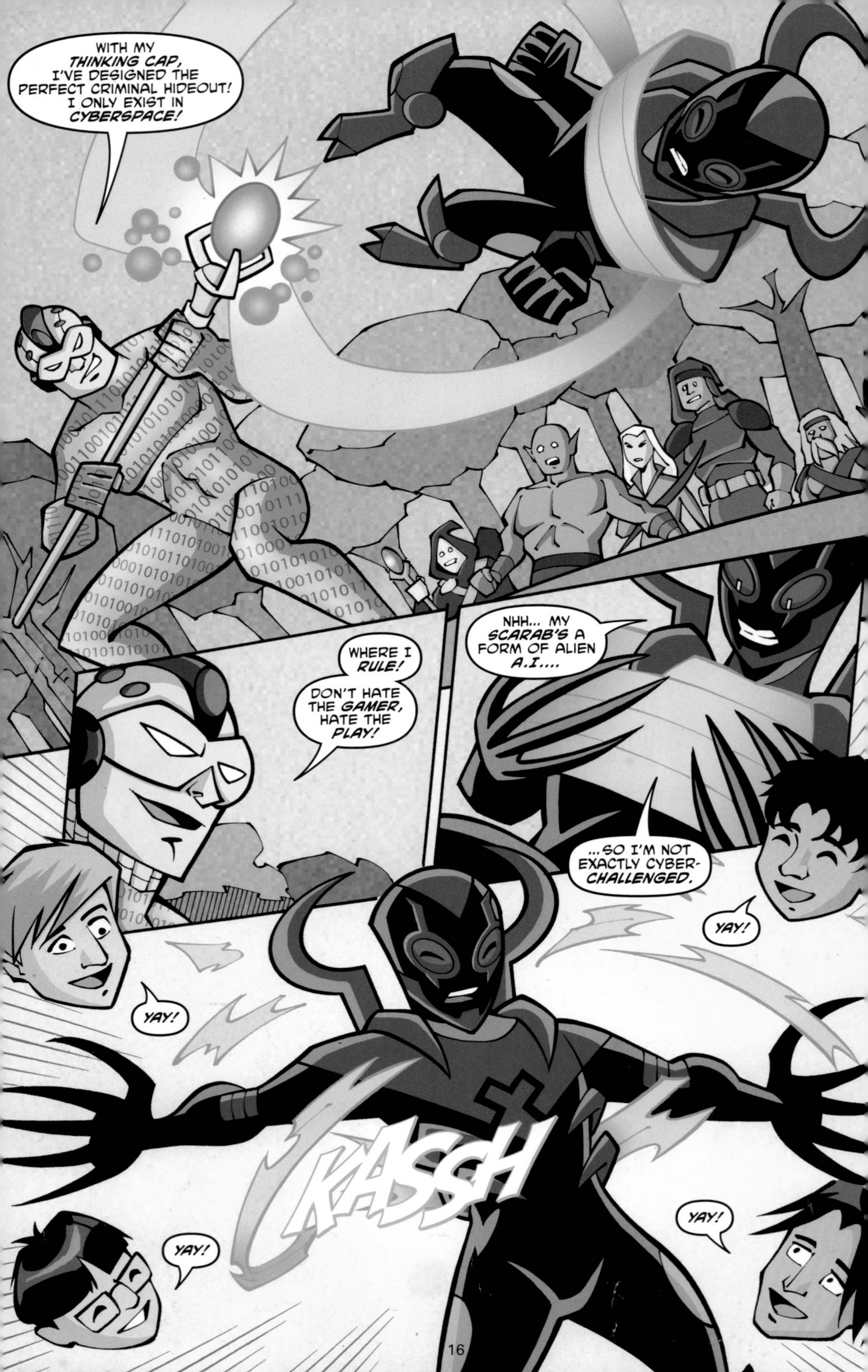
WITH MY THINKING CAP, I'VE DESIGNED THE PERFECT CRIMINAL HIDEOUT! I ONLY EXIST IN CYBERSPACE!
WHERE I RULE!
DON'T HATE THE GAMER, HATE THE PLAY!
NHH... MY SCARAB'S A FORM OF ALIEN A.I....
...SO I'M NOT EXACTLY CYBER-CHALLENGED.
YAY!
YAY!
KRASSH
YAY!
YAY!

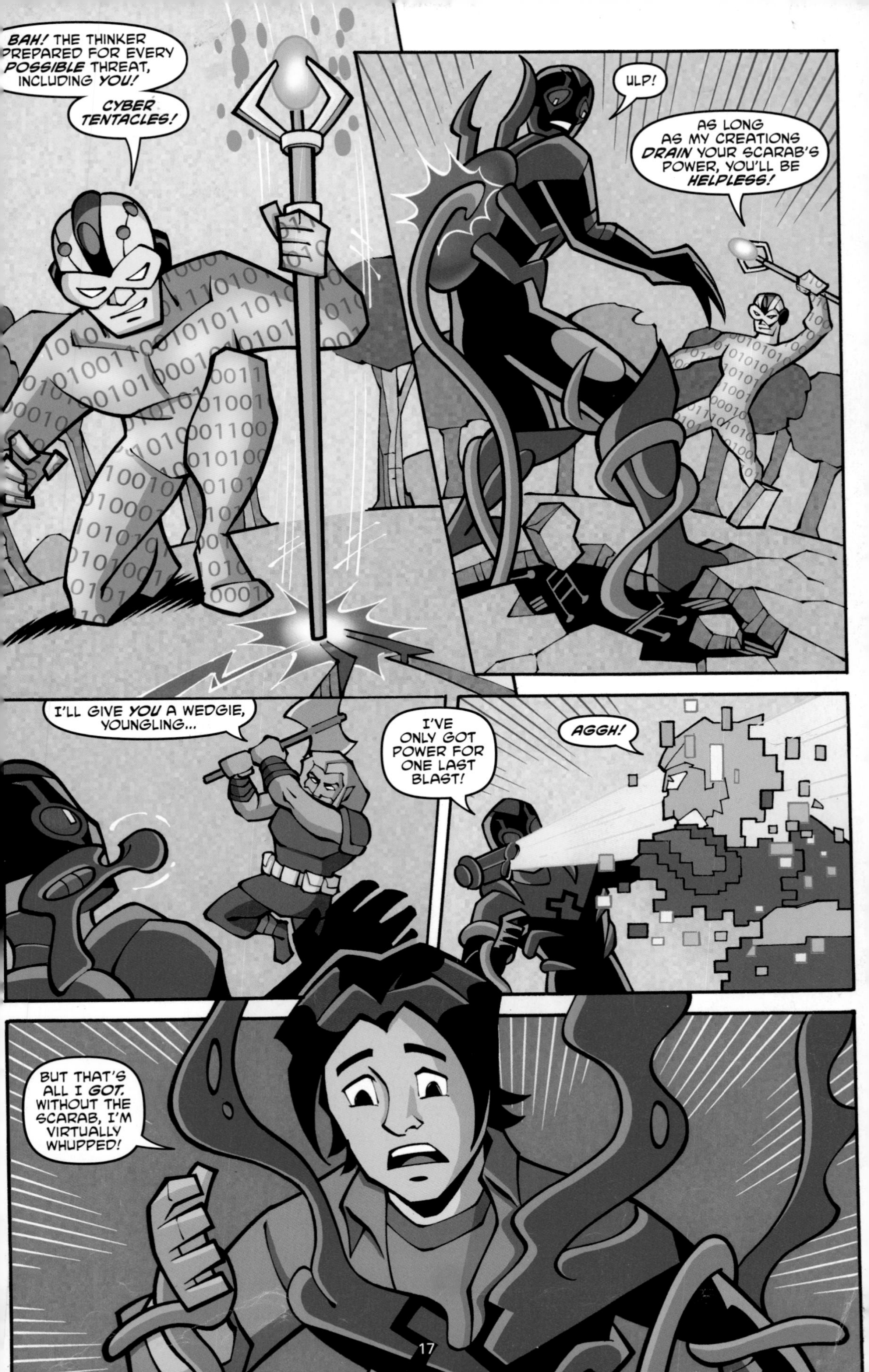
BAH! THE THINKER PREPARED FOR EVERY POSSIBLE THREAT, INCLUDING YOU!
CYBER TENTACLES!
ULP!
AS LONG AS MY CREATIONS DRAIN YOUR SCARAB'S POWER, YOU'LL BE HELPLESS!
I'LL GIVE YOU A WEDGIE, YOUNGLING...
I'VE ONLY GOT POWER FOR ONE LAST BLAST!
AGGH!
BUT THAT'S ALL I GOT. WITHOUT THE SCARAB, I'M VIRTUALLY WHUPPED!

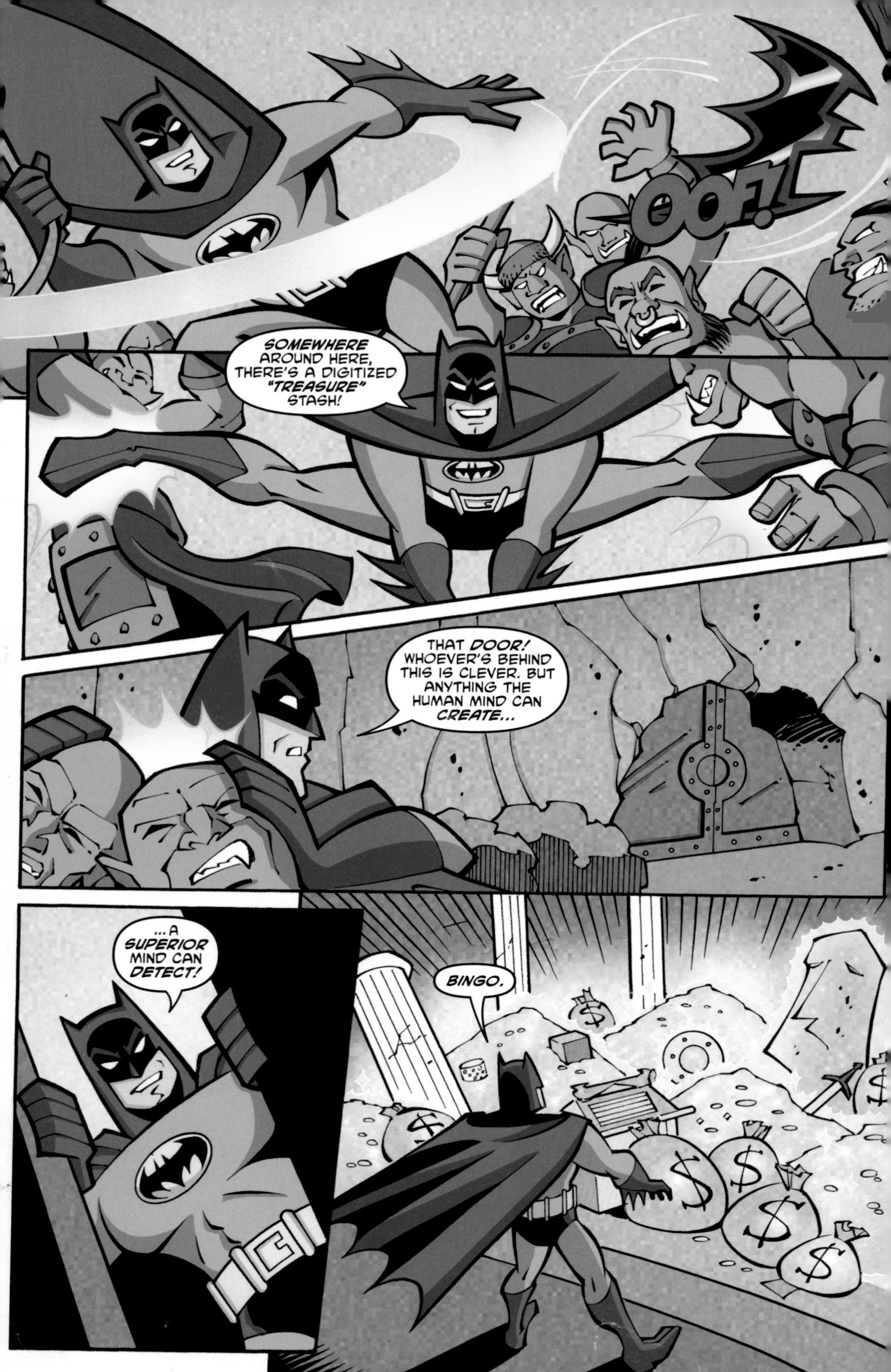
OOF!
SOMEWHERE AROUND HERE, THERE'S A DIGITIZED "TREASURE" STASH!
THAT DOOR! WHOEVER'S BEHIND THIS IS CLEVER. BUT ANYTHING THE HUMAN MIND CAN CREATE...
...A SUPERIOR MIND CAN DETECT!
BINGO.

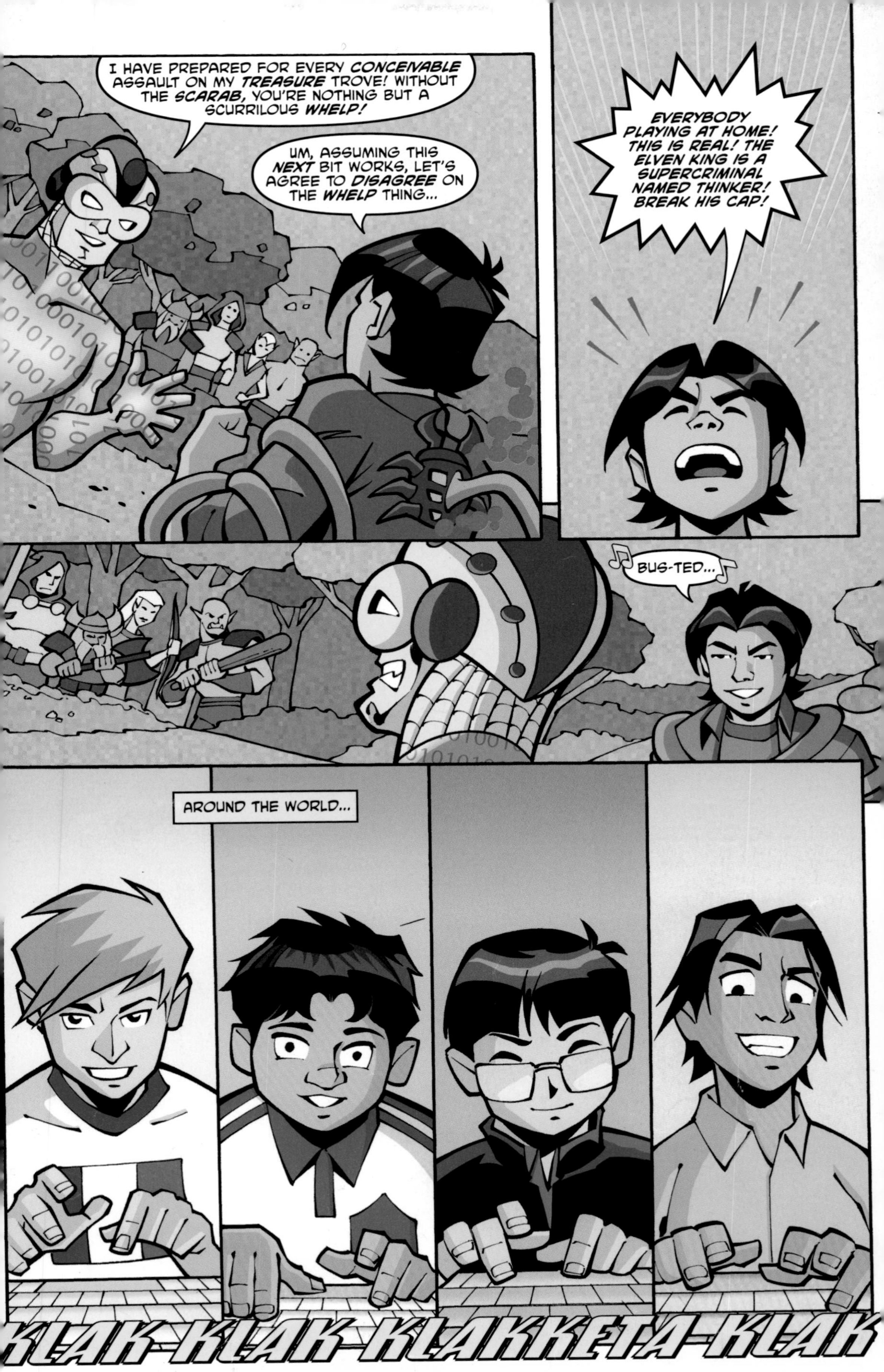
I HAVE PREPARED FOR EVERY CONCEIVABLE ASSAULT ON MY TREASURE TROVE! WITHOUT THE SCARAB, YOU'RE NOTHING BUT A SCURRILOUS WHELP!
UM, ASSUMING THIS NEXT BIT WORKS, LET'S AGREE TO DISAGREE ON THE WHELP THING...
EVERYBODY PLAYING AT HOME! THIS IS REAL! THE ELVEN KING IS A SUPERCRIMINAL NAMED THINKER! BREAK HIS CAP!
BUS-TED...
AROUND THE WORLD...
KLAK-KLAK-KLAKKETA-KLAK

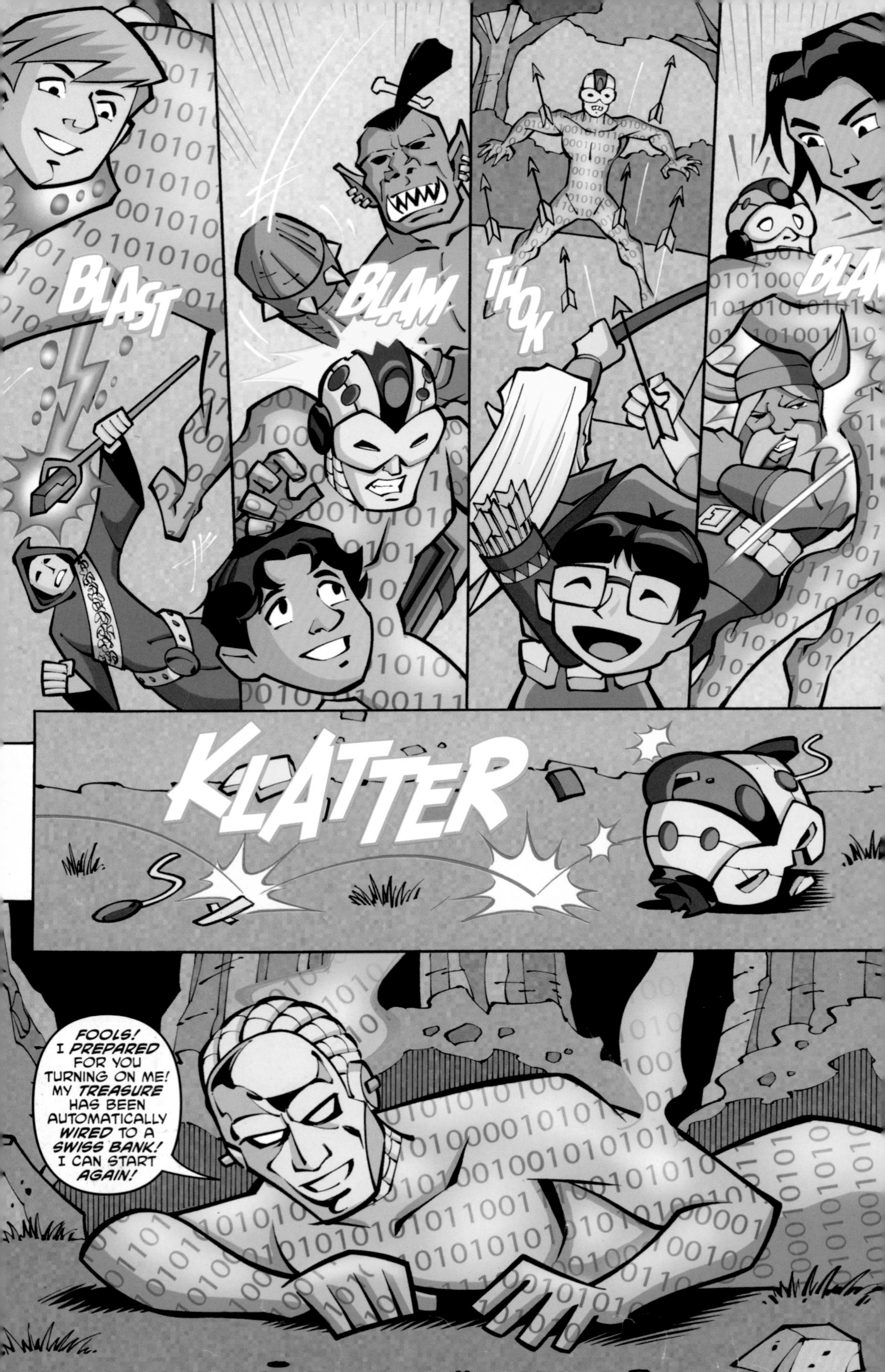
BLAST
BLAM
THOK
BLAM
KLATTER
FOOLS! I PREPARED FOR YOU TURNING ON ME! MY TREASURE HAS BEEN AUTOMATICALLY WIRED TO A SWISS BANK! I CAN START AGAIN!

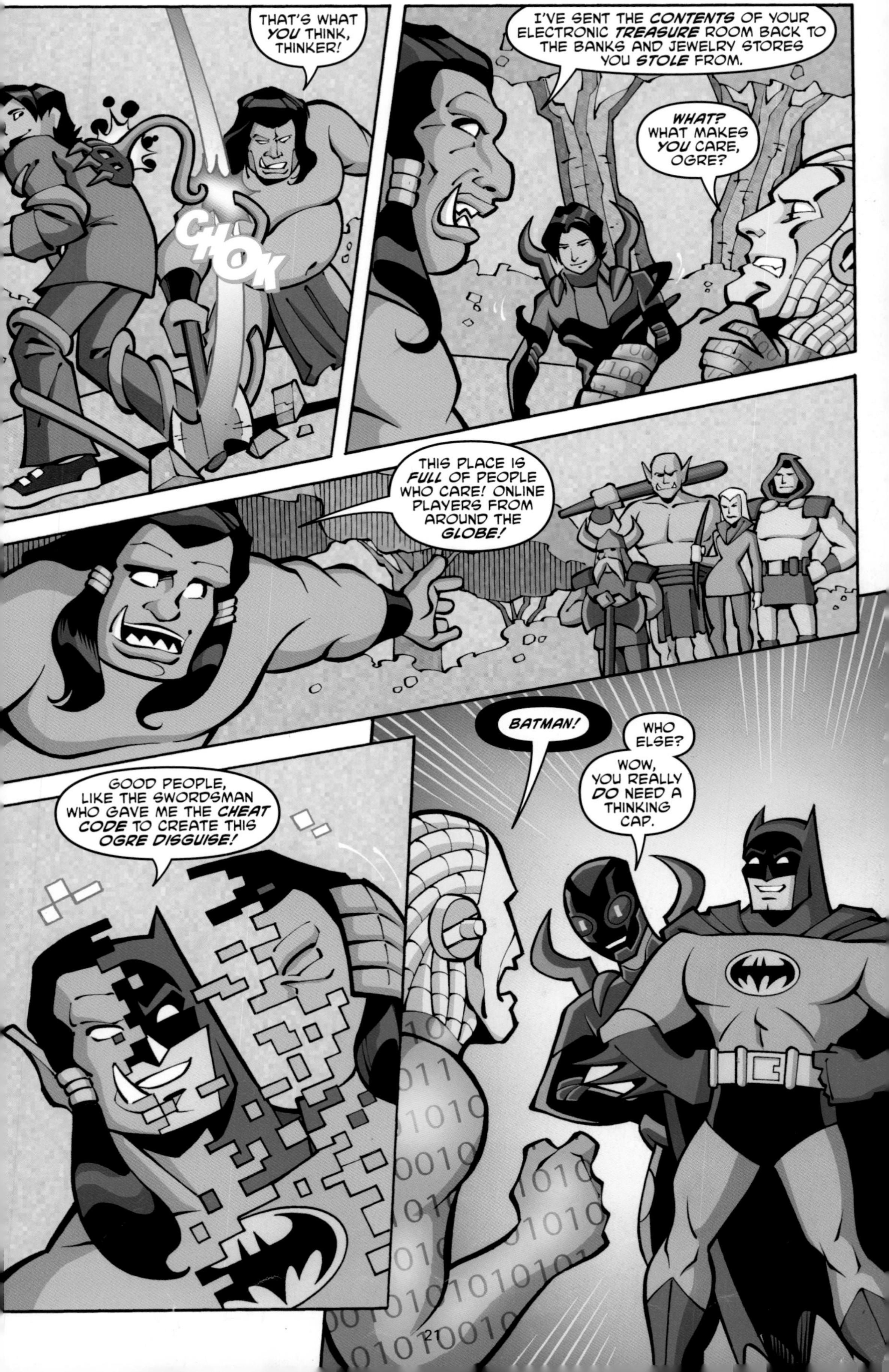
THAT'S WHAT YOU THINK, THINKER!
CHOK
I'VE SENT THE CONTENTS OF YOUR ELECTRONIC TREASURE ROOM BACK TO THE BANKS AND JEWELRY STORES YOU STOLE FROM.
WHAT? WHAT MAKES YOU CARE, OGRE?
THIS PLACE IS FULL OF PEOPLE WHO CARE! ONLINE PLAYERS FROM AROUND THE GLOBE!
GOOD PEOPLE, LIKE THE SWORDSMAN WHO GAVE ME THE CHEAT CODE TO CREATE THIS OGRE DISGUISE!
BATMAN!
WHO ELSE?
WOW, YOU REALLY DO NEED A THINKING CAP.

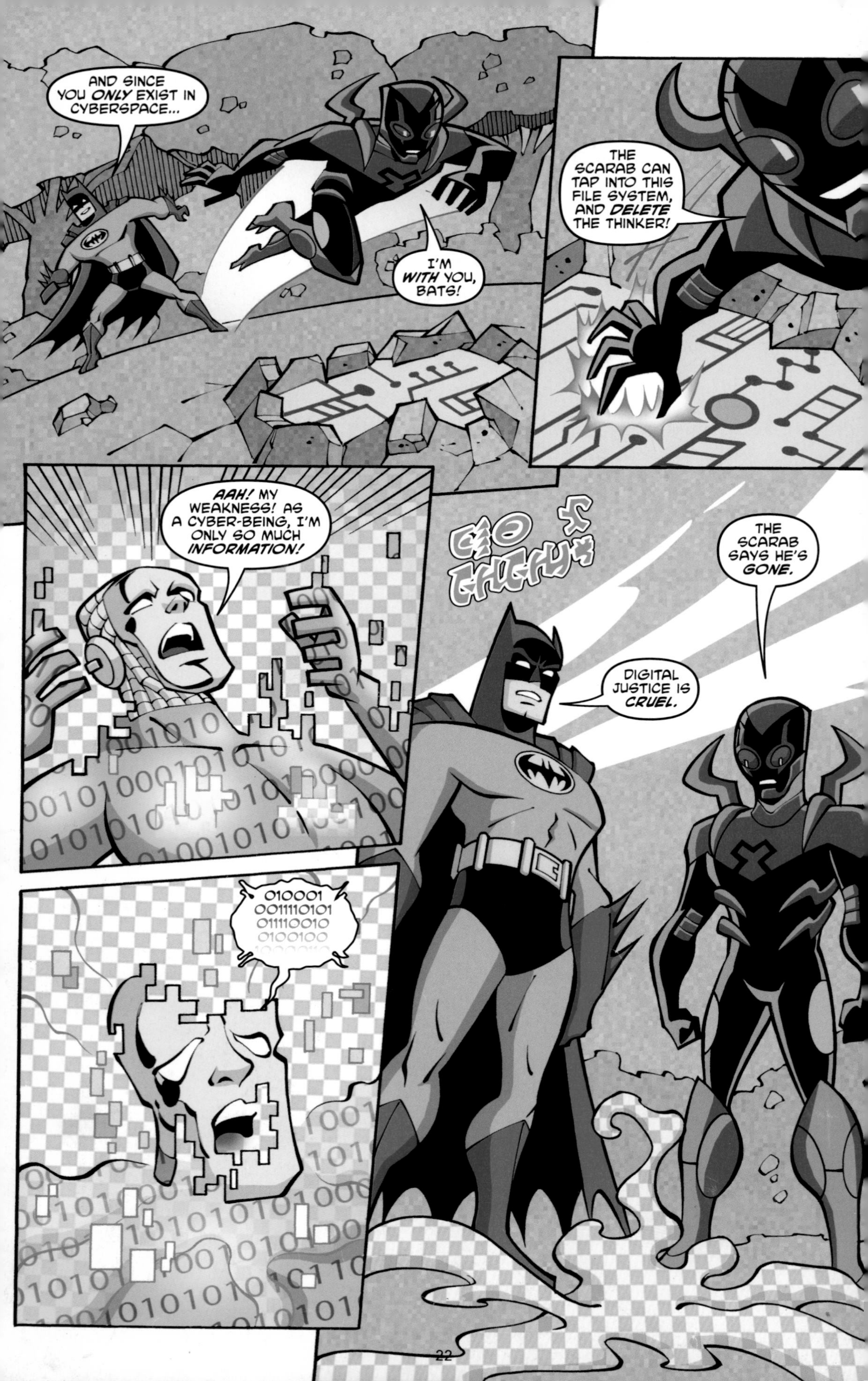
AND SINCE YOU ONLY EXIST IN CYBERSPACE...
I'M WITH YOU, BATS!
THE SCARAB CAN TAP INTO THIS FILE SYSTEM, AND DELETE THE THINKER!
AAH! MY WEAKNESS! AS A CYBER-BEING, I'M ONLY SO MUCH INFORMATION!
010001 0011110101 011110010 0100100
THE SCARAB SAYS HE'S GONE.
DIGITAL JUSTICE IS CRUEL.

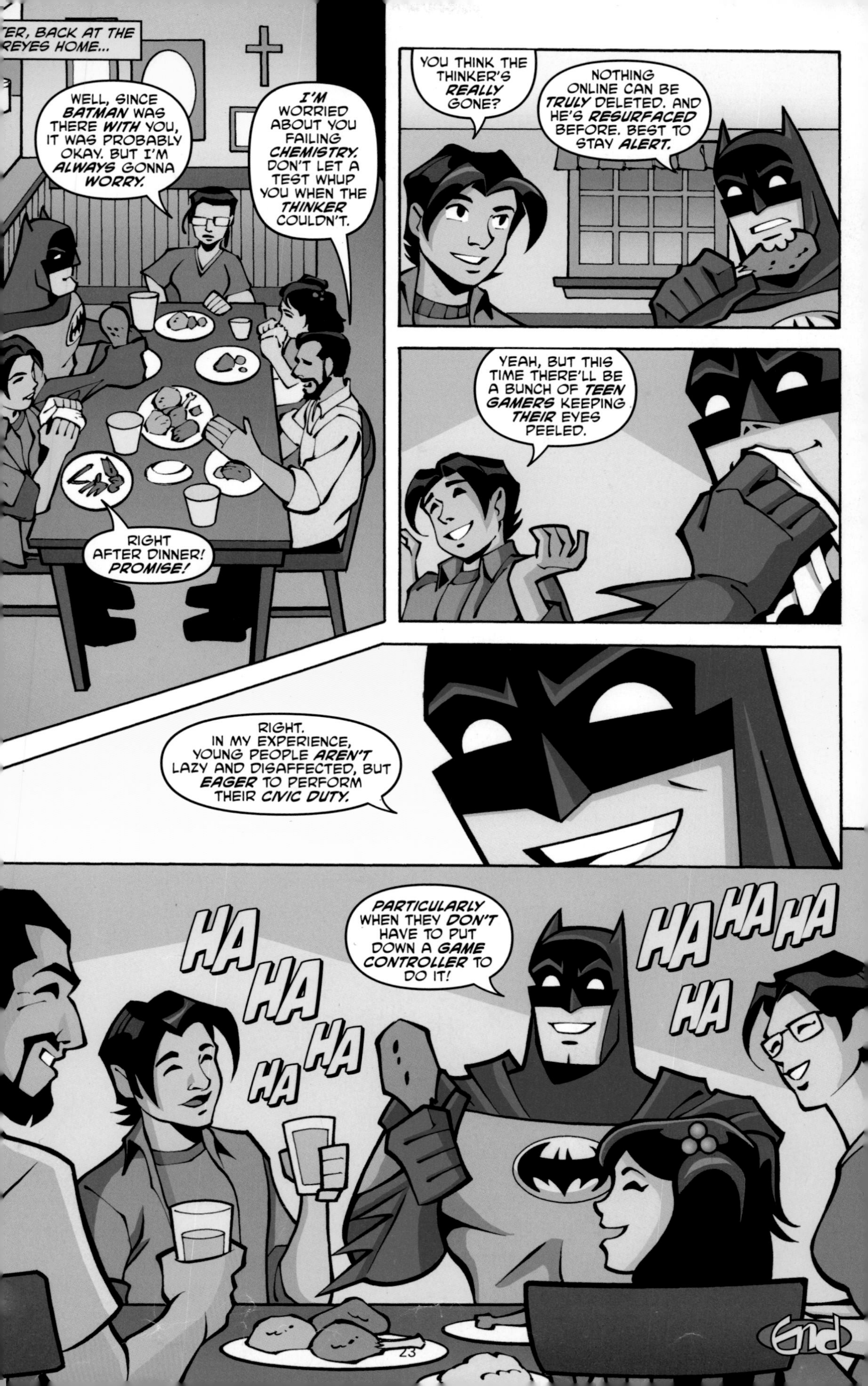

ER, BACK AT THE REYES HOME...
WELL, SINCE BATMAN WAS THERE WITH YOU, IT WAS PROBABLY OKAY. BUT I'M ALWAYS GONNA WORRY.
I'M WORRIED ABOUT YOU FAILING CHEMISTRY. DON'T LET A TEST WHUP YOU WHEN THE THINKER COULDN'T.
RIGHT AFTER DINNER! PROMISE!
YOU THINK THE THINKER'S REALLY GONE?
NOTHING ONLINE CAN BE TRULY DELETED. AND HE'S RESURFACED BEFORE. BEST TO STAY ALERT.
YEAH, BUT THIS TIME THERE'LL BE A BUNCH OF TEEN GAMERS KEEPING THEIR EYES PEELED.
RIGHT. IN MY EXPERIENCE, YOUNG PEOPLE AREN'T LAZY AND DISAFFECTED, BUT EAGER TO PERFORM THEIR CIVIC DUTY.
HA HA HA HA
PARTICULARLY WHEN THEY DON'T HAVE TO PUT DOWN A GAME CONTROLLER TO DO IT!
HA HA HA HA HA
End

THE THINKER

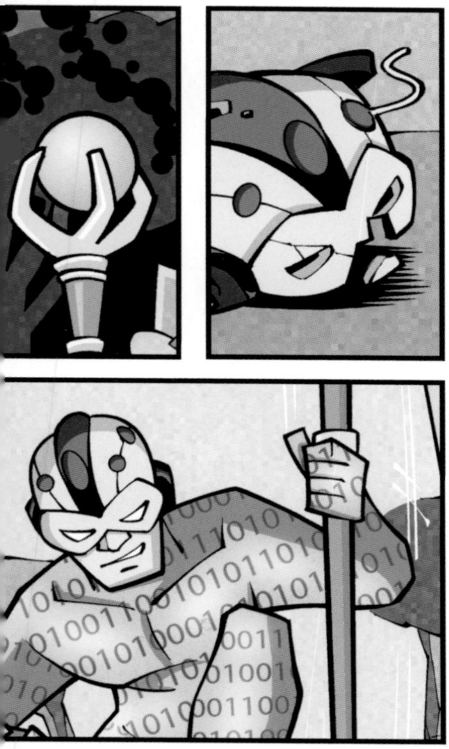

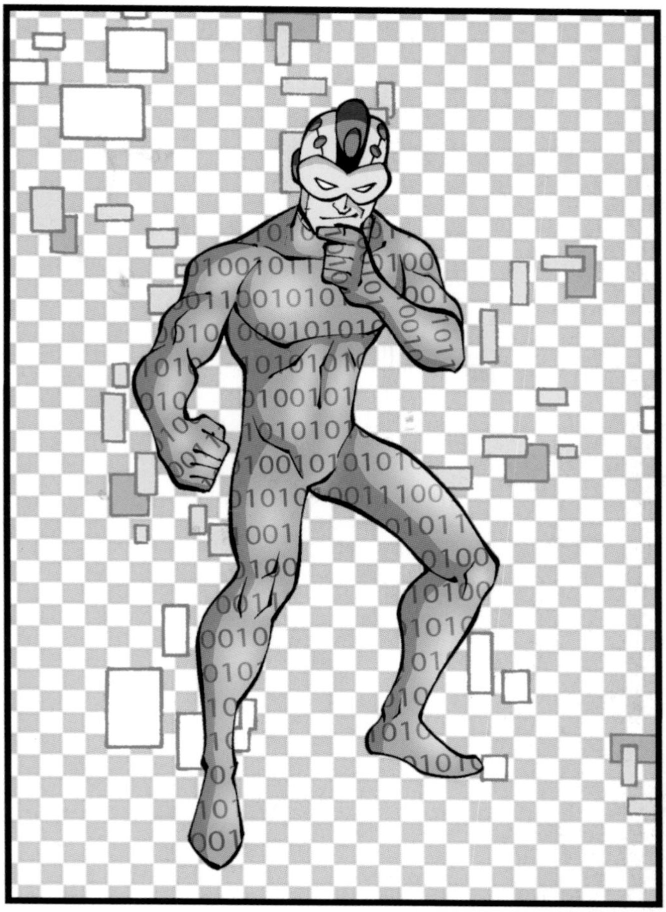

The Thinker stole his thinking cap from a government agency – the first of many bad ideas. He soon found his mental capacity greatly increased. But the villain still wasn't smart enough to turn down a life of crime.

TOP SECRET:

A heist gone bad left the Thinker without a physical body. He now only exists in cyberspace.

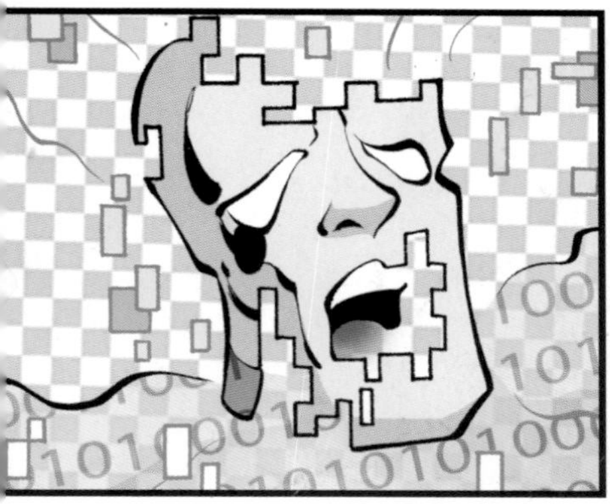

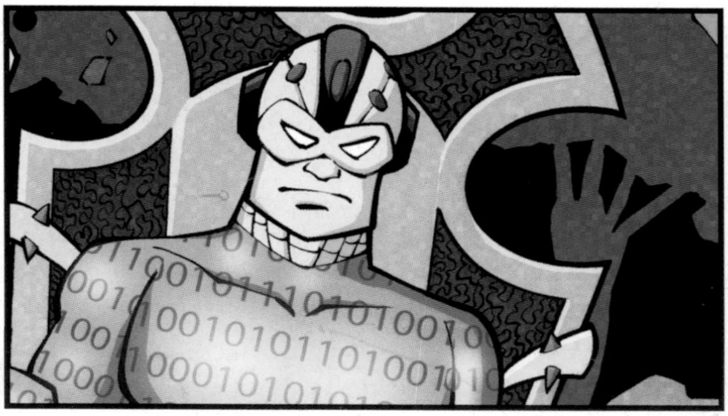

BLUE BEETLE

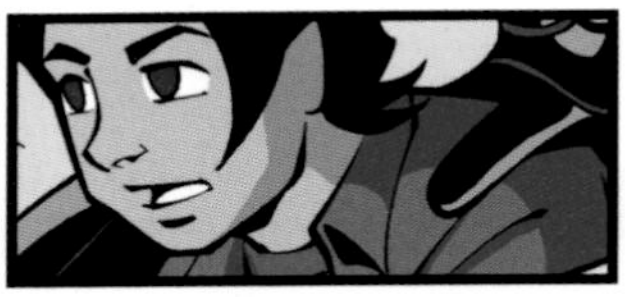

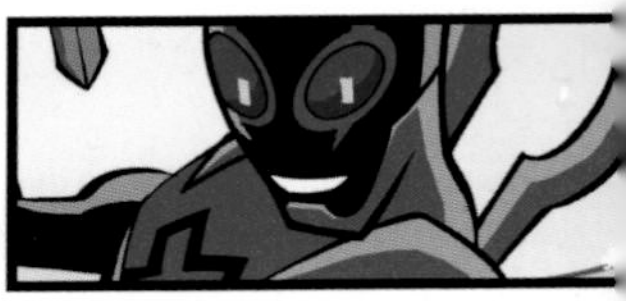

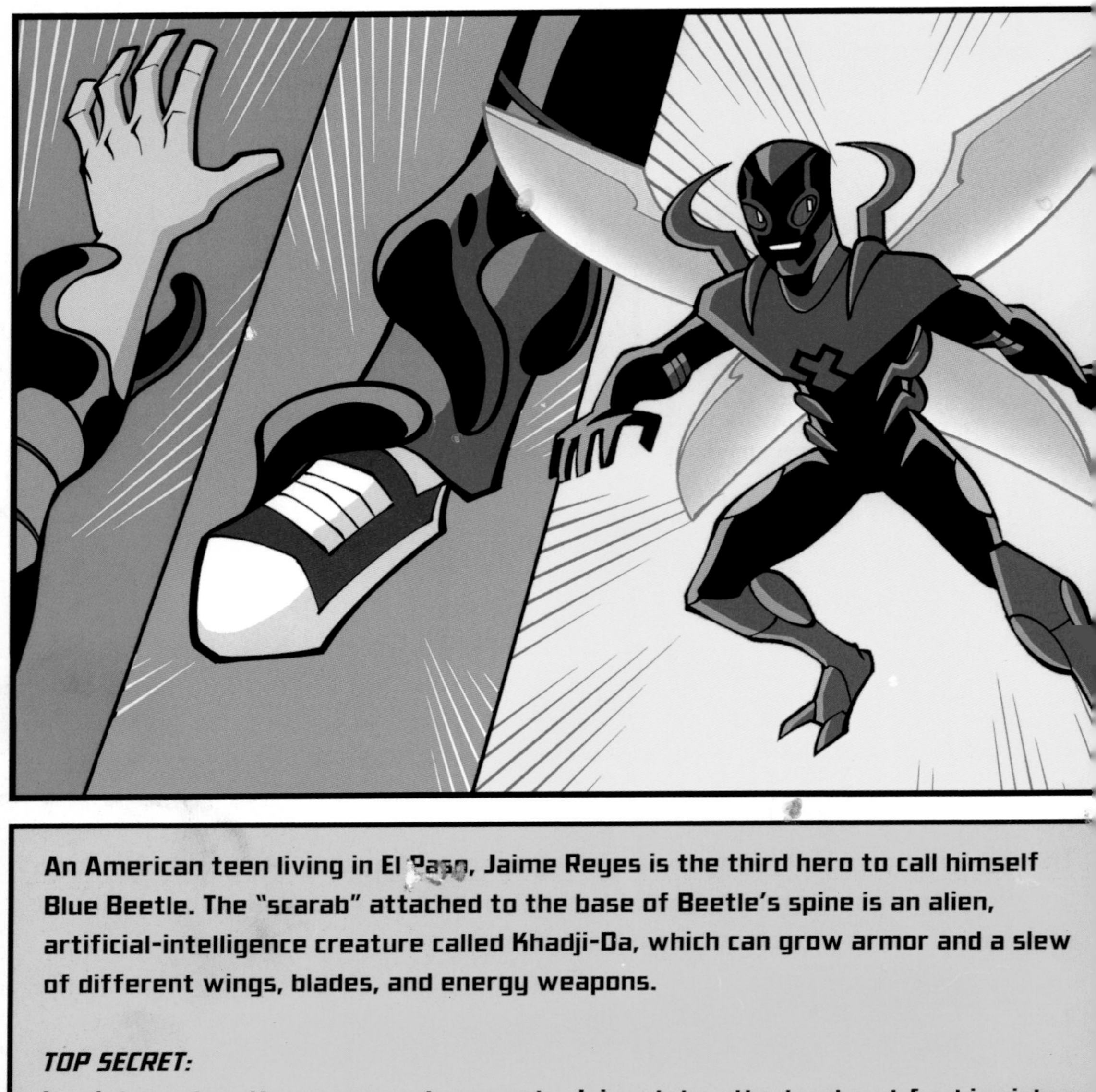

An American teen living in El Paso, Jaime Reyes is the third hero to call himself Blue Beetle. The "scarab" attached to the base of Beetle's spine is an alien, artificial-intelligence creature called Khadji-Da, which can grow armor and a slew of different wings, blades, and energy weapons.

TOP SECRET:
In winter, when the sun goes down early, Jaime takes the trash out for his sister, because she is secretly afraid of the dark.

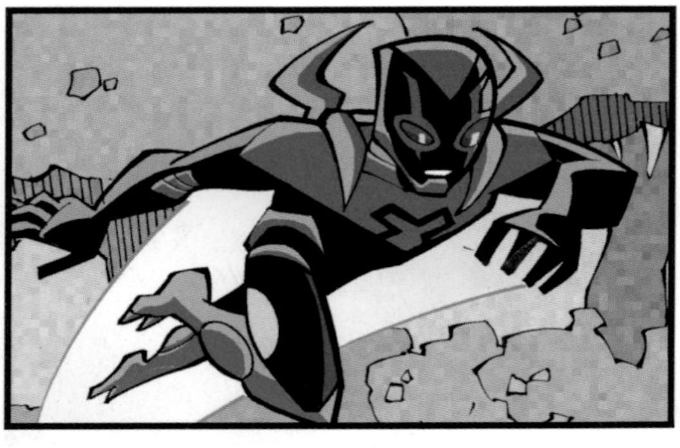

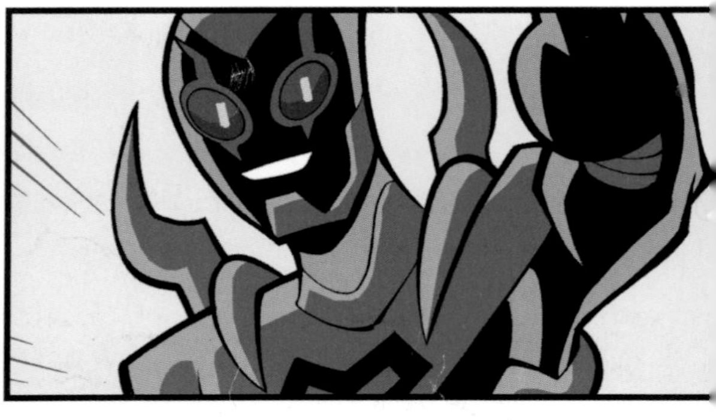

CREATORS

MATT WAYNE WRITER

Matt Wayne is a writer who has worked on TV series including *Ben 10: Ultimate Alien, Static Shock, Danny Phantom,* and the animated movie *Hellboy: Storm of Swords.* He was an editor at Milestone Media, and has written comics including *Hardware, Shadow Cabinet, Justice League Unlimited,* and more.

PHIL MOY ARTIST

Phil Moy is a professional comic book and children's book illustrator. He is best known for his work on DC Comics, including *Batman: The Brave and the Bold, DC Super Friends, Legion of Super-Heroes in the 31st Century, The Powerpuff Girls,* and many more series.

SCOTT JERALDS COVER ARTIST

Scott Jeralds is an illustrator of both comic books and animation. His credits include *Batman: The Brave and the Bold, Krypto the Superdog,* and more.

GLOSSARY

absorbed [ab-ZORBD] - very much interested in

confessions [kuhn-FESH-uhnz] - admissions that you have done something wrong

cyberspace [SYE-bur-spayss] - the environment of virtual reality

disintegrate [diss-IN-tuh-grate] - to break into small pieces

iconic [eye-KON-ik] - the ideal representation of a concept or thing

mechanical [muh-KAN-uh-kuhl] - operated by machinery

mortal [MOR-tuhl] - a human being

sayonara [sah-yoh-NAR-uh] - a Japanese word meaning "good-bye"

suspicious [suh-SPISH-uhss] - having the appearance that something is wrong or bad

VISUAL QUESTIONS & PROMPTS

1. You don't see the face of the evil villain in this story until page 20. However, there is a small clue on page 7 that shows what he looks like. Look at the panel. Can you find the clue? Did you notice it the first time you read the story?

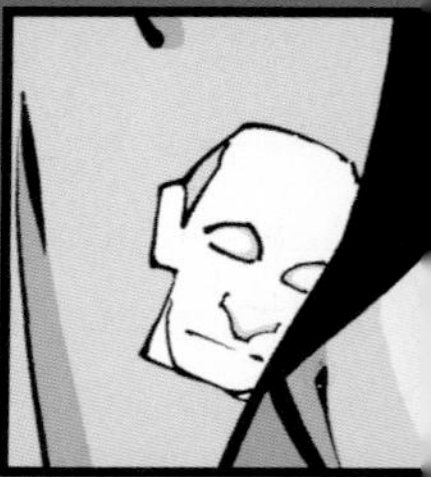

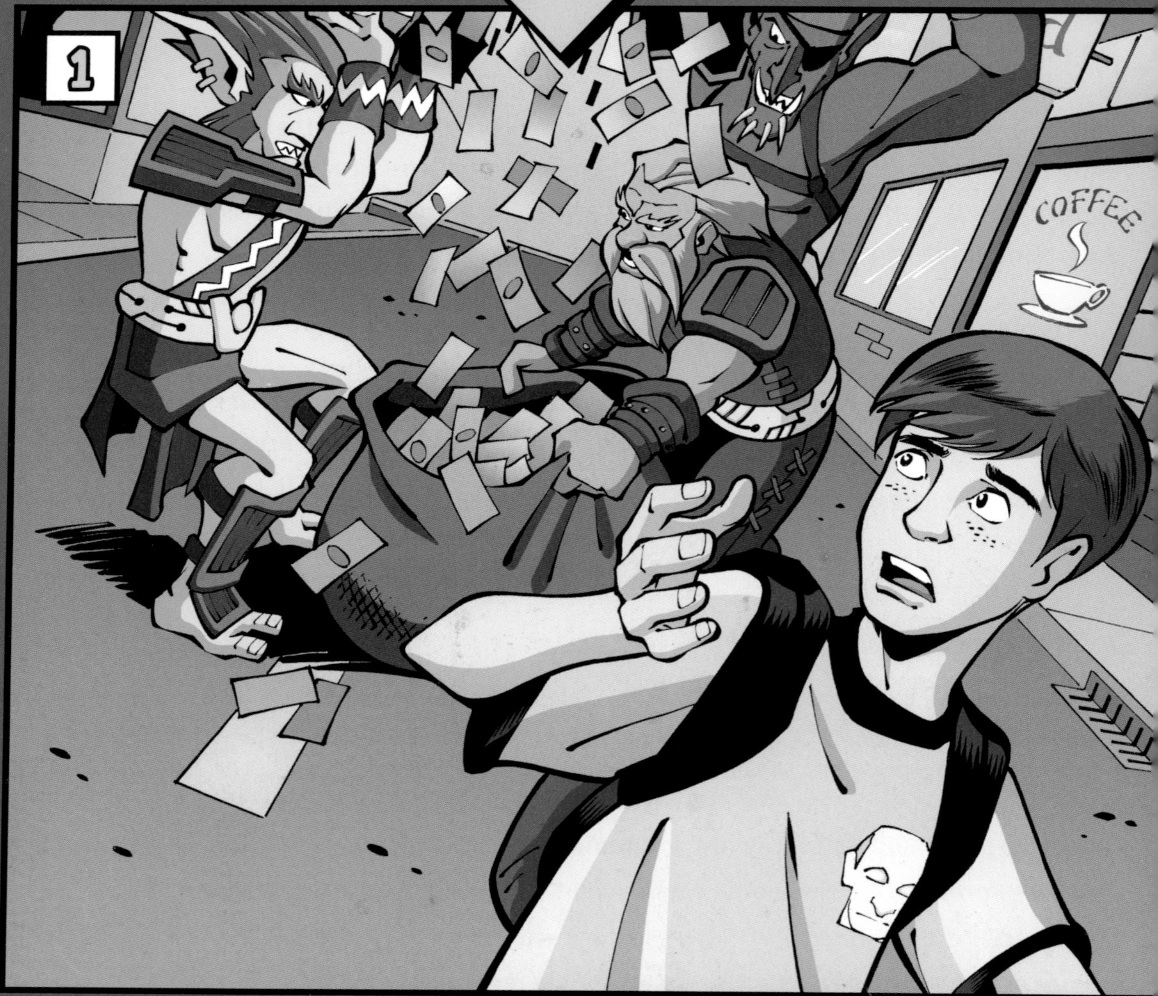
1
COFFEE

2. A character's expression can tell you a lot about how he or she is feeling. Look at the image. How do you think the worker is feeling? Why?

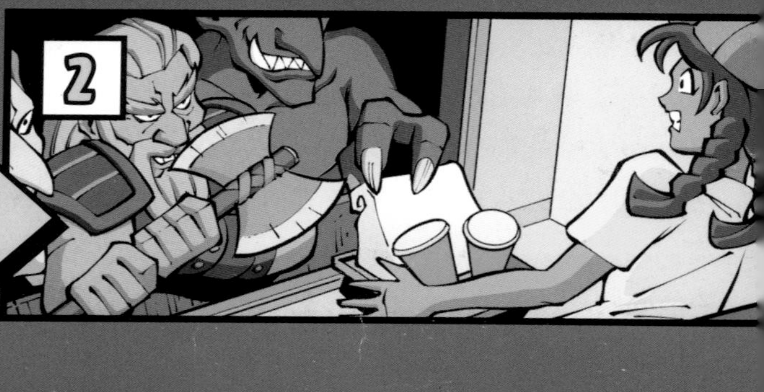
2

3. Most of the story takes place in Texas, but on page 15 you see boys from around the world. Look at each panel and find two clues that help show where each boy is from.

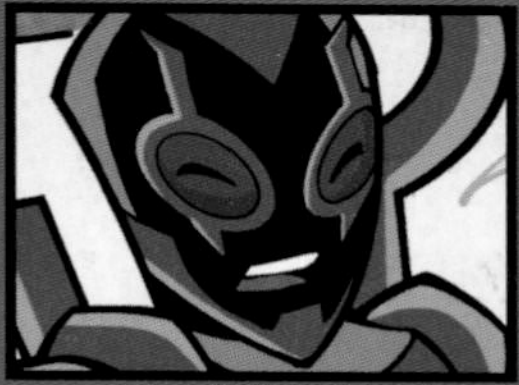

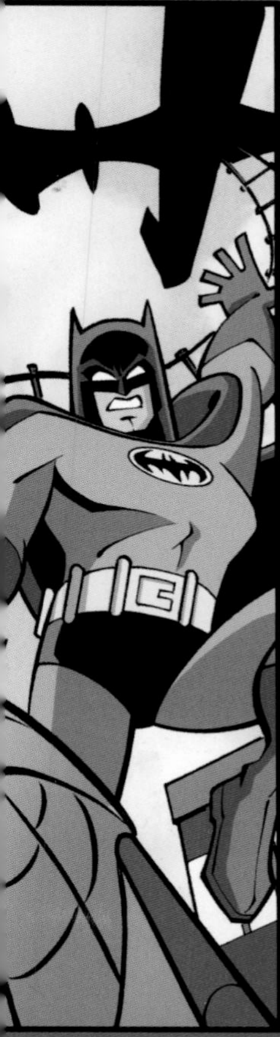

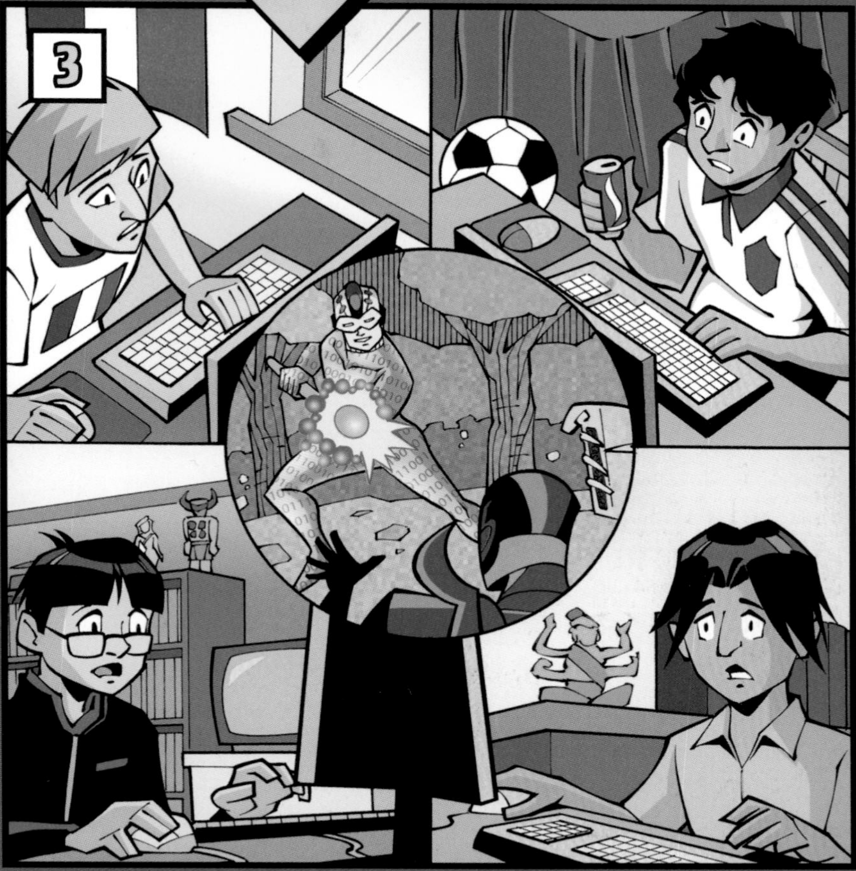
3

4. Did the billboard in the panel below give enough information for you to realize the villains were from a video game, or did you need the text to support the art? Explain your answer.

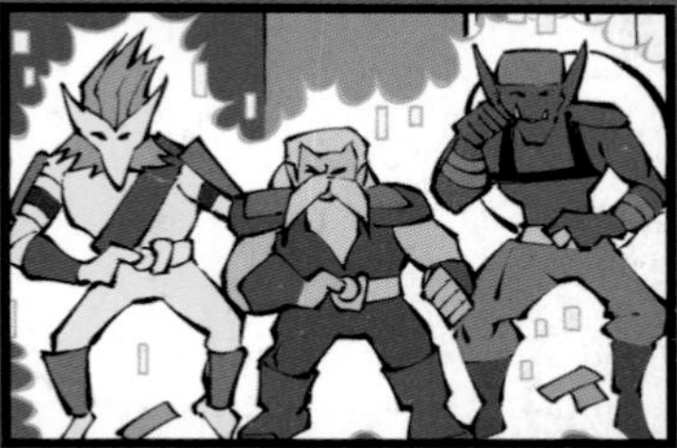

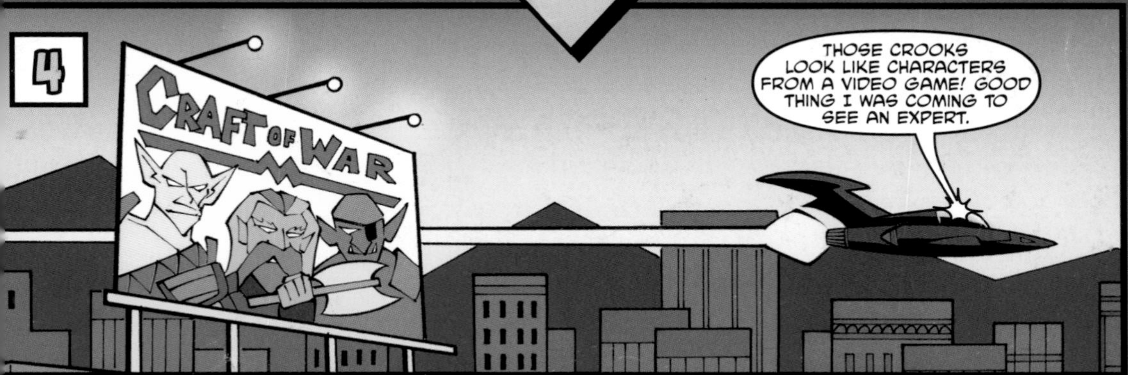
4
CRAFT OF WAR
THOSE CROOKS LOOK LIKE CHARACTERS FROM A VIDEO GAME! GOOD THING I WAS COMING TO SEE AN EXPERT.

READ THEM ALL!

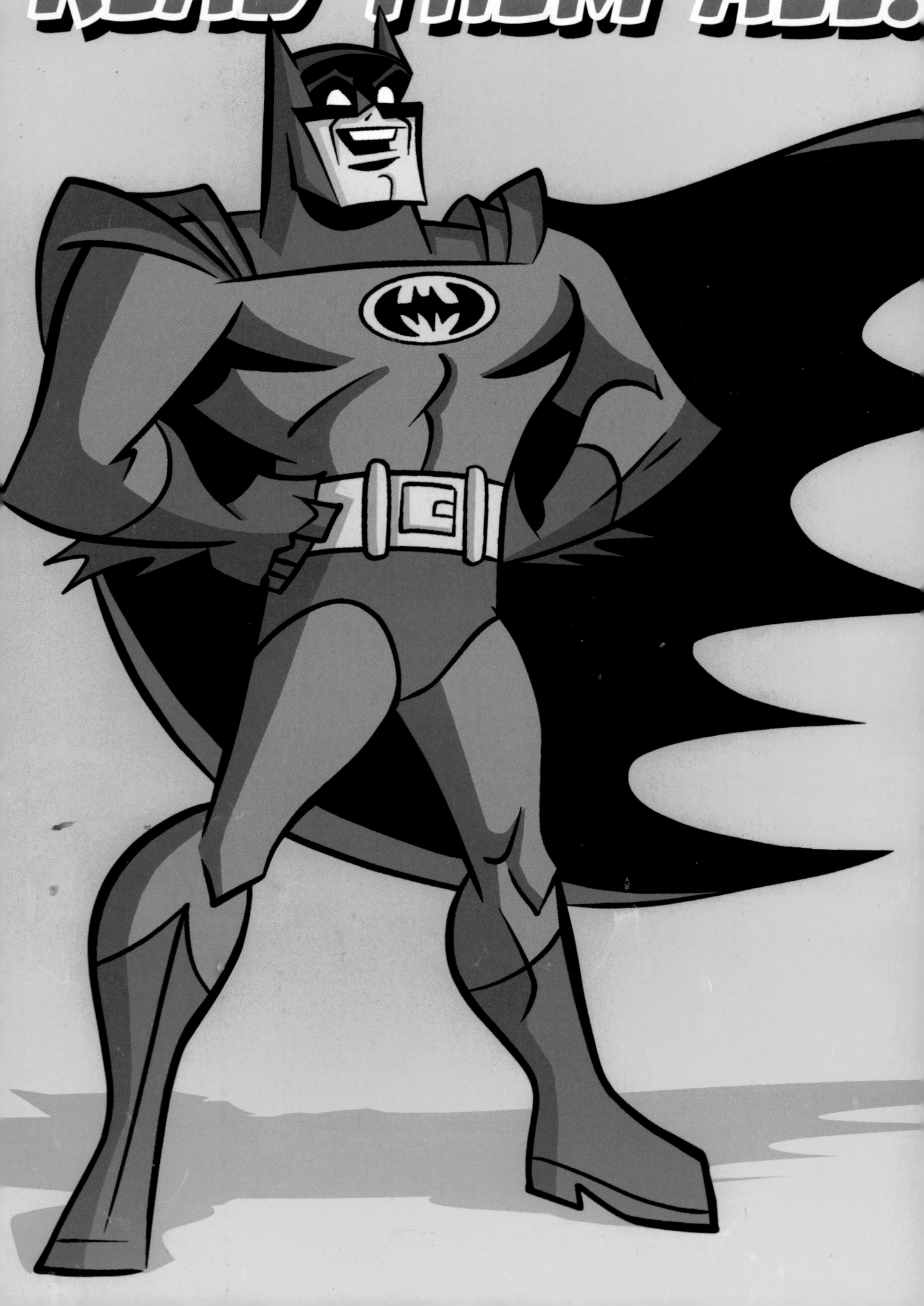

BATMAN
THE BRAVE AND THE BOLD®

DC COMICS
BATMAN
THE BRAVE AND THE BOLD
THE PANIC OF THE
COMPOSITE
CREATURES
WAYNE • SURIANO • DAVIS

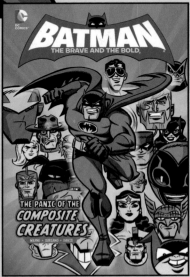

THE PANIC OF THE COMPOSITE CREATURES

BATMAN
THE BRAVE AND THE BOLD
THE ATTACK OF THE
VIRTUAL VILLAINS
WAYNE • MOY

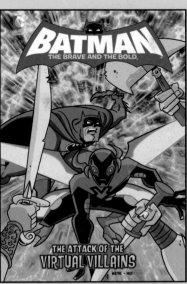

THE ATTACK OF THE VIRTUAL VILLAINS

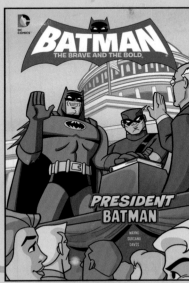

DC COMICS
BATMAN
THE BRAVE AND THE BOLD
PRESIDENT
BATMAN
WAYNE
SURIANO
DAVIS

PRESIDENT BATMAN

DC COMICS
BATMAN
THE BRAVE AND THE BOLD
MENACE
OF THE
TIME
THIEF
WAYNE
SURIANO
DAVIS

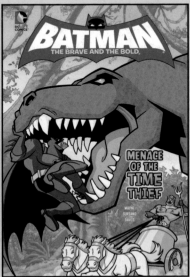

MENACE OF THE TIME THIEF

THE FUN DOESN'T STOP HERE!

DISCOVER MORE AT....

WWW.CAPSTONEKIDS.COM

THEN FIND COOL WEBSITES AND MORE BOOKS
LIKE THIS ONE AT WWW.FACTHOUND.COM.

JUST TYPE IN THE BOOK ID:
9781434245465

WANT EVEN MORE COMICS:

TO FIND A COMICS SHOP NEAR YOU:
CALL 1-888 COMIC BOOK
OR VISIT WWW.COMICSHOPLOCATOR.COM